**"You've paid a hell of a price
over the years for being
a little too beautiful,
a little too young,
a little too lonely."**

But he believed she had been unfaithful. Her stomach was suddenly churning with turbulent emotions. "Matthew, you think you understand—"

"No. Not understand. I'm trying to tell you that I don't give a damn. It's past...I'm not a boy," he said quietly. "And there would be no chance of your being unfaithful to me. Do you want me to show you?"

The fire was sending golden sparks up the chimney. There was no reason for the vulnerable little shiver that rippled through her body. "No," she whispered.

He was behind her, but she could feel his smile. His arms tightened around her, securing her in a cherishing, protective embrace. "Yes," he said softly. "Let me touch you. Let me show you..."

Dear Reader:

Spring is just around the corner! And we've got six new SECOND CHANCE AT LOVE romances to keep you cozy until it arrives. So sit back, put your feet up, and enjoy . . .

You've also got a lot to look forward to in the months ahead—delightful romances from exciting new writers, as well as fabulous stories from your tried-and-true favorites. You know you can rely on SECOND CHANCE AT LOVE to provide the kind of satisfying romantic entertainment you expect.

We continue to receive and enjoy your letters—so please keep them coming! Remember: Your thoughts and feelings about SECOND CHANCE AT LOVE books are what enable us to publish the kind of romances you not only enjoy reading once, but also keep in a special place and read again and again.

Warm wishes for a beautiful spring,

Ellen Edwards

Ellen Edwards
SECOND CHANCE AT LOVE
The Berkley Publishing Group
200 Madison Avenue
New York, N.Y. 10016

WINTERGREEN

JEANNE GRANT

**SECOND CHANCE AT LOVE
BOOK**

Other books by
Jeanne Grant

Second Chance at Love
MAN FROM TENNESSEE   #49
A DARING PROPOSITION   #149
KISSES FROM HEAVEN   #167

To Have and to Hold
SUNBURST   #18

WINTERGREEN

First edition published April 1984

First printing

"Second Chance at Love" and the butterfly emblem are trademarks belonging to Jove Publications, Inc.

Printed in the United States of America

Second Chance at Love books are published by
The Berkley Publishing Group
200 Madison Avenue, New York, NY 10016

CHAPTER
One

CAREFULLY, LORNA SLIPPED the key into the lock, yawned hugely, and tiptoed into the hall of her first-floor apartment trailing a chiffon scarf and a gold-spangled evening purse that seemed too monumentally heavy to lift at two in the morning.

"I thought I told you to stay out and have a good time."

Lorna jumped, her head pivoting around toward the scolding voice. Freda Noonan had a hand on one hip and was all wide-awake, foot-tapping impatience. Lorna shook her head, suppressing a tired smile. As a daunting image, her friend lacked something. Freda's red-gray hair was in curlers, and she was wearing a robe the Goodwill would have rejected a decade ago. "The sun's about to come up. I thought you wouldn't mind if I came home," Lorna said dryly.

"*Don't* tell me you were worried about Johnny."

"Of course I wasn't." Lorna hesitated. "But he was okay, wasn't he? This afternoon I thought he was coming down with a cold..."

"Between your Johnny and my Brian, the house

1

was destroyed three times over. Mostly *your* monster's energies. Which is the point," Freda chided. "Potential father material. What was wrong this time?"

"Nothing," Lorna said mildly. "Hal has a lot of potential wrestler in him, but except for that he seemed fairly law-abiding. Why on earth did you wait up for me?"

"God knows. You're getting beyond help," Freda said disgustedly.

Lorna grinned and pushed back a dark mane of chestnut hair as she kicked off her sandals. "You want wine or coffee—as in, how long is this scold going to take? Keep in mind that both boys will be up at dawn."

"Wine, and for the rest of the night the boys are your problem. Why do you think I decided to baby-sit here tonight? And don't be sending my little angel next door any earlier than ten tomorrow morning."

Lorna chuckled, moving through the pale green living room that she knew had some claim to taste and even serenity . . . somewhere beneath the model airplanes and comic books. Switching on the overhead light in the kitchen, she wondered for a full second and a half if it was worth the effort to drag a chair over to reach the wineglasses in the top cupboard. It wasn't. She poured the Pinot Noir into two Pac Man mugs, aware that Freda had trailed after her.

"Honey, he was gorgeous. And don't try to tell me he wasn't interested."

"Oh, he was interested," Lorna agreed. "The so-called bash at his place had a massive guest list of four, and the other couple politely left at eleven."

"I thought you said . . ."

"I did. I thought it was going to be a big affair."

"All right. So what happened between eleven and two?" Freda demanded interestedly as she picked up her mug of wine.

"Nothing unusual. First we played sophisticated seduction. You know, how many times can he fill my glass while we talk. Then he shifted to poker, as in, let's see if I was *really* bluffing when I said no. Then we had to check out whether I was the kind who liked a man to be a little rough." Lorna's voice was full of dry humor, as she automatically cleaned up the children's glasses and took a swipe at the counter with a damp sponge.

"And *then*..." Freda prompted impatiently.

Lorna took a sip of wine and perched up on the counter, her dark gray eyes rueful as she met her next-door neighbor's gaze. "And then...nothing. I just told him that I'd honestly had enough, and the chase came to an end rather abruptly. Hal turned into a lamb..." Lorna considered. "Maybe not exactly a *lamb*..." At Freda's quelling stare, Lorna's humor subsided, her smile fading.

"Lorna, I thought you liked him," Freda said despairingly.

"I do."

"And you can't tell me you weren't attracted—"

"He's very good-looking," Lorna agreed.

"Well, then?"

Lorna sighed, her thick dark lashes suddenly shielding the vulnerable cloud-gray of her eyes. "Couldn't you see the way Johnny looked at Hal when he came to pick me up? He didn't like him, Freda. And Hal just isn't kids-oriented." Lorna hesitated. "Maybe farther down the road, Hal might even have offered a ring, but I have a feeling the next day he'd have been looking into boarding schools."

"Lorna, he couldn't have spent more than an hour with the boy! You can't live your entire life through Johnny. With your looks, you've got a right to be picky, but honey, you're downright impossible. And that boy needs a father before you ruin him completely. *Someone* has to have the courage to land a good one on his backside occasionally."

"I know that. In principle, I'll even grant that Johnny needs a masculine influence. The problem is that the men who make good fathers turn me on like dead dishrags. Say, Freda, are you going home soon?" Lorna inquired politely. It wasn't as if they hadn't covered the territory before.

"Obviously, I might as well."

Lorna slipped down from the counter and finished her wine, setting the mug down by the sink. "You were a sweetheart to watch the two of them."

Freda moved to the back door. "It balances out; you know that. Brian's here more than he's home." She paused with her hand on the doorknob and turned back to Lorna. "You don't still have Johnny's father on your mind? Lorna, you've got to trust again. Everyone isn't like that Whitaker clan—"

Something cold and familiar settled in Lorna's throat, but she shook her head with a weary smile. "I haven't thought of a Whitaker in nearly nine years. Don't be silly, Freda."

"You've waited a long time—"

Lorna whispered firmly, *"Go home."*

The door closed with a little click, and Lorna let out a pent-up sigh, raking her hand restlessly through her hair. After locking the back door and switching off lights, she headed toward the bedrooms, her hands unconsciously reaching behind her to unzip her dress. The first door was Johnny's, and she automatically peeked in.

Freda's son Brian was stretched out peacefully, the covers snugged up to his chin. Predictably, her own son was another matter. His blankets had been pulled out from the bottom of the bed and were trailing on the floor along with his arm, and only one leg was covered. Lorna silently rearranged the blankets, taking a moment to smooth the irrepressible cowlick on top of Johnny's towhead and to kiss the freckles he hated. Both worry and love showed on her expressive face as she tiptoed back out, leaving the door open an inch or two.

He was too smart, her nine-year-old son. In fact, his school had identified him as a gifted child. He was also stubborn, curious to the point of being insatiable, courageous to the point of recklessness, and at times, Lorna admitted to herself, he was more than she could handle. Last week there had been more trouble at school...

The dress slipped down from her shoulders and made a silky pool on her bedroom carpet. No one was going to tattle if it stayed there until morning. The makeup, though, had to come off. Her eyes were burning from the layer of mascara applied too many hours before.

In the bathroom, she creamed the makeup off her face, brushed her teeth, and then took a brush to her shoulder-length hair. Unsmiling, she viewed her image in the mirror. Almond-shaped gray eyes stared back at her, large and dark-lashed. Her classical features were surrounded by a thick mane of dark red-brown hair that crackled under the hairbrush. Her figure was long-legged and long-waisted, her high breasts barely contained in a pale green camisole. She made no particular claim to beauty, but at twenty-nine she would have been foolish not to admit she had the kind of looks that attracted men. Knowing that brought Lorna no special pleasure. Her looks had netted her one husband named Richard Whitaker once upon a time; indirectly, those same looks had been responsible for losing him. But she didn't want to think about Richard; she didn't want to think about any of the Whitaker men. The only Whitaker who concerned her was one towheaded little urchin named Johnny.

She turned away, flicking out the light. Moonlight flooded the bedroom, casting long silver waves on the pale yellow comforter. She crawled into bed and curled up, though she knew she was too restless to sleep. Her worries about Johnny refused to go away. Other single parents seemed to manage just fine. Why couldn't she? Freda was so positive that a man's influence was all Johnny needed. Self-discipline wasn't exactly a characteristic of nine-year-old boys, and Lorna was definitely not famous for her iron hand. When Johnny acted up, her urge was always to give him more love instead of more discipline, if only to make up for his not having a father.

Unfortunately, Johnny inhaled that love the way a sponge soaked up water, and then exhaled trouble. He was violent in every way. Violently loving, violently protective, violently defending his point of view until he was violently convinced he was wrong. Then he would perversely, and just as violently, stick to his guns.

Lorna smiled in the darkness, closing her eyes. She adored her son. But who ever heard of a fourth-grader being kicked out of school?

You've got to *do* something, her conscience ordered. The problem was *what* to do. There were so few options . . . A Whitaker face whirled in her head. The face was that of Richard's brother, Matthew. She sent it furiously right back down to her subconscious. It resurfaced. She buried it again.

The image of Matthew Whitaker would never have come to haunt her if Johnny weren't a Whitaker in every temperamental little bone in his body. Like should know what to do with like. Who else but a Whitaker could understand the family characteristics?

Richard had been dead a long time, and hell would freeze over before Lorna turned to either his father or his brother for help. But Johnny had needs that she couldn't fulfill either emotionally or financially, and that reality was no small blow to her pride and fierce spirit of independence. The Whitakers had it all—money, power, a respected name—and Johnny was the only heir. Surely he had certain rights...

Irritably, Lorna punched the pillow and ordered herself to settle down. She didn't know why she allowed herself to dwell on the subject of the Whitaker family.

The Whitakers didn't believe that Johnny was Richard's son. And they never would.

It was almost two months later that hell froze over. Literally, Lorna thought crossly as she did her best to control her ancient Camaro, which was bucking in the wind. She tried not to see the violent weather as a bad omen.

She'd grown up in the shadow of the University of Michigan where her father was a professor, and the attachment she felt to the small town of Ann Arbor was strictly a sentimental one. She loved it. Huge old brick buildings, ivy-covered, reeking with character and tradition, stood on tree-lined streets that climbed the gently rolling hills. In summer, the landscape was English-garden green; in spring, small blossoming trees sent out their fragrances in the shadow of larger oaks and maples; in winter, the snow piled up in Tudor doorways and casement windows with the picturesque quality of a Norman Rockwell painting.

But it happened to be autumn at the moment. November. And the landscape had nothing of the picturesque about it.

The snow was the kind that bit and stung, lashing at anything in its path. Angry gray clouds swirled in restless low masses, bringing on darkness as early as four in the afternoon. The massive old trees were stripped bare; dark, lampless windows added to the aura of gloom; and no one was venturing out for a casual stroll. The wind was so vicious that it was all Lorna could do to maneuver her small car, and by the time she had parked it her hands were shaking from their long, tight grip on the steering wheel.

As she emerged from the Camaro, the wind tossed up her chestnut hair and sleet assaulted the tender skin of her face. Her toes were already freezing in the tan leather sandals. She had chosen her outfit thinking only of her meeting with Matthew; the weather had been the last thing on her mind. Now she realized her folly: The leather gloves weren't warm enough; she wore no hat; her toes were growing numb; and, shivering violently in the lightweight tawny coat, she thought ruefully of the furlined parka at home in the hall closet.

She crossed the parking lot with her head bent and her arms crossed over her chest. Her stomach was churning up the five cups of coffee she'd had since morning, and three aspirins hadn't touched her headache. Looming ahead was a gray stone building with a sign: WHITAKER AND LAKER. The last time she'd seen it the sign had read WHITAKER AND WHITAKER. Brothers. The thought did nothing to settle her nerves. She took a deep breath and stepped inside.

Silence. Not only was there suddenly no lashing wind, but she'd forgotten how forbiddingly quiet an attorney's office could be. Unconsciously, her gloved hand clenched into a fist at her side as she glanced around. The decor had changed since Richard Whitaker, Sr. had retired. Conservative gold carpeting led up to a receptionist's desk; wildlife prints hung in exact symmetry over deep leather chairs in the lobby.

The redhead at the front desk, who looked up as Lorna entered the office, wore a gray pinstripe dress with a white collar.

Determinedly coming up with a smile, Lorna approached the paragon in gray, her hands ridiculously tight on her black crocheted shoulder bag. "I wonder if it would be possible for me to see Mr. Whitaker this afternoon?"

The redhead raised perfectly plucked eyebrows. "Do you have an appointment?"

Why did she bother to ask? Lorna thought dryly. We both know I don't. "Please tell him that Mrs. Whitaker is here."

Those perfect eyebrows vaulted upward. "I wasn't aware . . . Actually, Mr. Whitaker is in court. I was expecting him back an hour ago, but there's no way I can immediately contact him. I don't know what to tell you . . ." The receptionist hesitated, clearly having no idea what to do with a woman who claimed to have the same last name as her boss.

"May I wait?" Lorna asked patiently.

"Why . . . yes, of course."

Alone in the stark, tiled bathroom off the lobby, Lorna took a brush from her purse and restored order to her wind-tossed hair. Her cheeks were so red that she looked like Cherry Ames, and her lips were scarlet. Rapidly, she restored her appearance with lipstick and powder, adding a subtle hint of perfume. Her hands, to her annoyance, were trembling. The image in the mirror didn't please her. The pale blue dress now seemed all wrong. The oval neckline showed her collarbones; the bodice clung too closely to her breasts; and the navy piping at hem and cuffs . . . it was just wrong, that was all. Pinstripes with a white collar would have been appropriate. Unfortunately, she'd always hated pinstripes . . .

So just walk out if you're so damned scared, she told her reflection. Vulnerable gray eyes suddenly telegraphed an S.O.S. in the mirror as Lorna admitted to herself that she hadn't really planned very well what she was going to say to Matthew. To ensure Johnny's future she'd make her pitch from a street corner if necessary. Her nervousness wasn't the result of stage fright. It was the thought of seeing Matthew again that made her so tense.

He was a tough man, the kind who played to win and never backed down on a principle. Richard had modeled himself after his older brother; knowing that had intimidated Lorna when she first met Matthew. But until the end of the marriage, Matthew had always—oddly enough—had a soft spot for her . . . She had to hold that thought.

With a determined step, she opened the door to the bathroom and quietly walked into the lobby, not glancing at the receptionist. She sat down in one of the leather chairs, crossed her legs, stared out the window, and ordered herself to relax.

"Mrs. Whitaker?"

The redhead was suddenly standing in front of her.

"I think you'd be more comfortable in Mr. Whitaker's office," she said firmly. "I'll get you some coffee."

"Really, I'm fine," Lorna told her, but the redhead appeared to be accustomed to herding people. She'd evidently decided that a relative of the boss should be treated as such, even if she had never heard of the existence of a female Whitaker. Lorna found it impossible to explain that she wasn't positive Matthew would even talk to her, much less allow her near his inner sanctum.

Which was where she found herself standing, playing with the handle of her purse, several seconds later. Matthew's desk was a smooth slab of teak, spotless and gleaming. Lawyerly tomes filled the floor-to-ceiling shelves behind it, thick leather volumes that added to the elegance of the silent office. She took in the dark blue carpeting and teak paneling—very plush, very expensive. A pair of cream-colored leather chairs faced the desk; a long antique credenza stood behind them. The room was tasteful and quiet, but just being there increased the almost desperate feeling of dread in Lorna's heart.

For generations, the Whitaker men had dedicated themselves to the law, and Matthew was the best of that breed. Nine years ago, Richard had been a year out of law school; Matthew, five years older, had already been at the top of his profession. He hadn't wasted any time. He could have used the family influence to further his career, but he hadn't bothered. Matthew was not only a successful lawyer, but a pillar of righteousness; he was a one-man band on the black and white of justice. Richard had both idolized and resented him...

"Here we go."

Lorna pivoted as the redhead entered behind her, carrying a small tray. The sugar bowl and creamer were Waterford crystal, and the teaspoon was sterling silver. Whitaker traditions. The throbbing in Lorna's temples increased. At the moment, her bank balance was so low that she couldn't afford to pay a nickel to see the Statue of Liberty tap-dance.

"Sit down, please, Mrs. Whitaker. Really, it should only be another few minutes until Mr. Whitaker gets back. My name is Irene. Call me if you need anything..." The receptionist arched her eyebrows curiously, clearly hoping to learn Lorna's first name. Presumably, it would look better to the boss if she was on first-name terms with his relatives.

Lorna sighed mentally. "Lorna," she supplied simply.

The woman was satisfied, her smile radiant. "Well, then, Lorna, if you should need anything at all..."

She didn't. Irene propped the door open and left Lorna in peace for another fifteen minutes. That peace was shattered, however, by the low, husky baritone she hadn't heard in so very long. There was suddenly the strangest rushing in her ears, blocking out all other sounds.

Nine years ago, Matthew had been the one who'd severed all contact between Lorna and the Whitakers. She wasn't likely to forget his voice.

He was informing the redhead that his mother had been dead for twenty years, that he believed she knew he was unmarried, that there were no living female Whitakers, and that he was too damned tired to entertain imaginative women.

And then, suddenly, he was there; the redhead, flustered and flushed, just behind him. Lorna barely had time to stand up. He stopped midstride; Lorna knew he'd been prepared to oust the intruder from his office. Instead, he stood stone-still when he saw her.

Lorna had once known him well, yet still she faltered. He was taller and leaner than Richard, his body made up of more sinew than flesh; Matthew had never stood still long enough for any extra weight to settle on him. His gray suit jacket hung open over wide shoulders, and his steel chest was encased in an impeccable white shirt. Thick brown hair brushed his shirt collar and framed a square face with an iron chin, a high forehead, and dark brown, almost black eyes—cruel eyes, she thought fleetingly, though never before had they seemed cruel to her.

To others, yes. It was said that he could make a truthful witness stumble on the stand, that he could make the most articulate of judges stammer. The deeply etched lines on his brow only accented the strength of his face. She knew those lines. She saw them in

Johnny. It went beyond the perseverance that was a Whitaker family trait. Maybe Matthew couldn't make a mountain cave in with that look of his, but he could probably come close. No give, she read, and suddenly felt exhausted.

"You were right, Irene; I apologize," Matthew said suddenly. He turned to the redhead. "I won't need you anymore this evening."

CHAPTER
Two

"You're in trouble?"

"I . . . not trouble exactly, Matthew." As an opening speech, it lacked something, because that seemed to be the end of it. So much anxiety, so much adrenaline pumping, so many raw nerves . . . she had been prepared for an angry tirade and the gentleness of his questions had taken her by surprise.

"Sit down, Misha. Just tell me about it," he suggested quietly.

She leaned back in the chair and glanced up at him. No one but Matthew had ever called her Misha. She had been christened Mishalorna; her great-grandfather had been Russian, and her father had taught the language. But the name had lasted no longer than her infancy. Lorna was so much easier. Richard, especially, had always objected to the exotic hint of foreign name.

Matthew hadn't, and a very long time ago his special diminutive had always sounded teasing and affectionate. Now the sound of it sent a swift, strange rush of warmth through her. She grappled with the cool, distant speech she had prepared in her head. "I'm sure you feel I haven't any right to be here, and I promise I won't take up much of your time. If you'll just hear me out—"

"You haven't changed."

He was studying her, his eyes skimming over her crossed legs and supple, slim body, apparently assessing the difference nine years had made. His jaw seemed to tighten as he took in soft red lips and expressive gray eyes, the way she brushed her hair back from her forehead, the pale blue knit dress gently molded to her figure.

Disconcerted by his intimate survey, Lorna glanced down and tried to compose her thoughts again. It wasn't as if he could honestly be happy to see her.

"Misha? Are you going to tell me why you're here?"

"Yes. Of course." The thing to do was to get it over with. Lorna focused deliberately on the sheen of the teak desk rather than on those unfathomable eyes of his. There was no way she was going to let this drag on any longer than it had to. "The last time I saw you, Matthew, I was in the hospital. If you remember, you offered me a check for ten thousand dollars from . . . Richard."

The room suddenly seemed plunged into silence. She saw Matthew's impenetrable mask drop; the pulse in his throat was working overtime. Neither of them could forget that day, her son just born and Richard unwilling even to see her again; Matthew visibly upset by the role he was supposed to play in getting rid of her. She could still remember Matthew's face, the color of ash; the sterile white hospital room; her own shock and despair and the tears that just kept coming. What did you expect? Matthew had demanded. God, Misha, stop it. Why wouldn't you let me help you before it was too late?

He remembered. She could see it in his eyes. "I

hope," he said in a low, harsh voice, "you've got a damned good reason for bringing it up again. I know at the time you didn't have the sense to cash the check."

"No." She met his eyes squarely. "But I need the money now, Matthew."

He just stared at her, his whole body taut and tense. "Misha, Richard's been dead for more than eight years. Forget the past for a moment and just tell me what kind of trouble you're in." He gave the order quietly, even gently, but it was clearly an order nonetheless.

Lorna shook her head, her hands feeling suddenly shaky. "Matthew, I don't want anything from you," she said in a low voice. "But Richard felt he owed me that money. I could have had it then; it was mine." She swallowed. Her eyes, grave and anxious, never left his. "Demanding something for nothing isn't my style, Matthew. The thought makes my stomach turn over. But I felt...that was a debt. Your brother—"

"What was between you and Richard had nothing to do with me. I don't want to hear about it, Misha."

She'd been expecting just that glacial tone when he first walked in. Not now, after he'd seemed so open... Matthew at his most impenetrable was all ice. She knew he was like this in court, even with his family sometimes, but never before had he been so cold toward her.

His brows were knitted together as he studied her. Then gradually his forehead smoothed out as he watched her eyes cloud with distress. "Misha," he said gently, "I told you a long time ago that you could always come to me if you were in trouble. There's no reason to bring the past into it. Just tell me..."

She leaped up from her chair, crossing her arms under her breasts defensively as she walked to the window. His voice had changed from ice to velvet, and a strange sensation shivered down her spine. She'd never thought of Matthew as anything other than an older brother in her short year and a half of marriage, yet seeing him again after all this time . . . It was different, that was all. She just couldn't seem to feel the same way. He was not her brother-in-law, not anymore, yet he was still the man she'd shared so much laughter with many years ago. He'd helped her out of that shell of shyness Richard had had so little patience with. Confused for no reason, she touched her fingertips to her temples.

"Misha?"

She turned. "I need the money for Johnny. For my son."

It was as if lightning had suddenly struck the room; she could feel the close atmosphere of sudden storm, the threat of thunder . . . and knew she'd been a fool to come here. Her nerve endings suddenly tensed up like a thousand rubber bands stretched taut.

"For help with your son?" Matthew echoed coldly. "Dammit, Misha, how the hell could you have come here about the child? Maybe I could have done something before—you're the one who shut me out then . . ." Ebony eyes stared at her, and his voice grew lower. "Unless you've already been to the boy's father—"

Her nerve endings snapped then. "No, I haven't been to the boy's *father*," she ground out. "And I wouldn't have, even if Richard were still alive." Swooping toward the leather chair, she snatched up her purse, her hands trembling and her eyes taking on fire. "And I shut you out *then*, Matthew, because you wouldn't have listened. Any more than your brother listened, or your father." She shook her head wildly, whipping back her chestnut hair. "By that time, I'd had all I could take of the other Whitaker men. I just couldn't take abuse from you, too, Matthew. You're so right, all of you. So black-and-white *right*. You should all have been judges, not merely attorneys. Passing sentence on the rest of humanity from your nice little pedestals—"

"Misha—"

"I don't care what you think anymore. If it weren't for Johnny, I wouldn't have come back here in a thousand years—" Matthew had ripped open the old wound, and the pain seared through her as she remembered the agony of one long, desperate day after another so many years ago. They had charged her with adultery, and she'd had no way to prove her innocence . . . but it shouldn't still matter. Richard was dead. The wounds made by his father's blistering contempt had scarred over. Only Matthew . . . She'd thought there was just a chance Matthew might believe her now. She should have known better, just from living with Johnny. A Whitaker never forgot or forgave an injustice. It came with the genes. And she was an idiot to have come here. Her eyes blurred with a disgusting film of tears.

Suddenly, she felt Matthew's persuasive grip on her shoulders.

"Look. Why don't you sit down for a minute—"

"Just leave me alone—"

"I'll leave you alone," he agreed quietly, and promptly didn't. All she wanted to do was get out of there, yet she felt the backs of her legs brushing against the chair, his hold on her shoulders just firm enough to force her down into it.

She could cheerfully have killed him. "I want to leave," she announced crisply.

"When you're in shape to drive," he replied. "At the moment, you're in a mood to take on pedestrians at a thousand miles an hour. I think not, Misha."

He walked behind her, and her fingers pressed so hard into her temples that they left dents. Behind her, she heard the chink of ice against glass. He held a drink in front of her. "No, thank you." He nudged her fingers firmly around the drink. "Matthew," she said irritably, "for openers, drinking and driving don't mix."

"Speaking as a driver, Misha, I'd take an inch of liquor in that stomach of yours over a mile of temper." He leaned back against his desk, dangling one leg over one edge. For an instant, his dark eyes glinted with amusement, and then didn't. "I never meant to upset you," he said quietly.

"It wasn't your fault." Matthew was staring at her; finally she managed to look away, her pulse beating erratically. He was *not* her brother-in-law now; she could not seem to remember exactly what it felt like to relate to him as a brother. "I shouldn't have come here," she said distractedly. "I never really expected you to say yes. I convinced myself that you would, because I knew you would honor your brother's debts, but it wasn't exactly a debt. Even then. Richard regarded the ten thousand dollars as payoff money—"

"I'll give you the money, Misha."

"But you never had anything to do with it. It's just . . . my father's dead . . . I have no one else to go to, and I told myself I didn't care if I looked like a fool. That I could at least try, and then if you said no, I could walk right back out again . . ." She stared at him as he lifted the glass of amber liquid to his lips. For the first time, she noticed how tired he looked. There were lines of strain around his eyes, one long streak of silver in his hair that hadn't been there years ago. She glanced again at the silver sideburns. They added a distinguished air to his virile good looks, yet she felt a curious pang that he actually looked his thirty-eight years. "I could have sworn you just said you were going to give me the money," she said absently.

"I did. I knew the moment I walked in and saw you here that whatever gave you the courage to come

here had to be really important to you. Do you want
to tell me over dinner, Misha?"

"I . . ." Her head whirled. "No, I can't, Matthew.
Johnny's waiting; there's someone taking care of him,
but I have to get back."

His jaw tightened at the mention of Johnny's name.
All the more reason why his request startled her. "So?
You were going home to eat anyway, and I haven't
eaten either. If you don't have enough food, I could
stop and pick up something . . ."

He waited. She hadn't the slightest idea what to
say. In the deepest part of her soul, she knew that
was exactly why she'd come, not so much for the
money as to talk about Johnny with Matthew. Because
he was a Whitaker, because he was . . . Matthew. Yet
she'd never really expected him to give her that op-
tion, feeling as he did about her, about his brother.
And Johnny was a reminder of that awful time . . .

"You're right, Misha," he said suddenly, as if he
could read her mind. He sighed, standing up and looking at her with weary, brooding eyes. "I have no desire
to see the boy," he admitted bluntly. "I don't even
know what prompted me to ask you to dinner, but
seeing you again and . . ." He hesitated, and his voice
suddenly went low and gentle. "I haven't forgotten
my brother. But that's not to say I ever thought he
was blameless. I can imagine what the last nine years
must have been like for you, raising a child alone,
losing your father. I read about his death in the paper,
Misha, and I'm sorry. More than once I worried about
what had happened to you."

"I've wondered about you, too," she said quietly.
She hesitated, slinging the purse over her shoulder
again. "But I never really expected you to forget what
happened between Richard and me." Her voice was
careful, the question in it almost unconscious.

"No."

"Of course not," she said swiftly, and stared at the door. "Well..."

"To forget something of that magnitude isn't possible, but then, to say I haven't changed in nine years would be just as foolish." He shrugged, just a little, a boyish gesture that made Lorna want to smile. "We used to enjoy quite a few dinners together, Misha. To make peace in the Middle East, reorganize Chrysler, and straighten out your misguided politics."

"*My* misguided—"

His teasing chuckle was tentative. "I was just kidding," he said gently. "There's no reason why it should be difficult for us to sit down to dinner together. I said you could have the money, Misha, and you can—no strings attached. But if you want to talk to someone about it—"

"I do. For one thing, I don't want you to think I want the money for some whim..."

Brilliant, aren't you? Lorna scolded herself as she pulled the Camaro onto the highway. Matthew's low-slung Morgan was directly behind her. Thanks to her big mouth.

A real friend would have committed her. Where were her real friends when she needed them? *Now* she remembered that Johnny was capable of taking an instant dislike to any man who walked in the door, that meat loaf was not exactly a gourmet dish fit for a Whitaker, that she had no tactful way to explain Matthew's last name to her son, and that the only thing she wanted to talk to Matthew about—Johnny—was the only subject that was clearly forbidden.

And Matthew... What he'd been thinking of, she just didn't know. She'd never really understood him. So often after she and Richard were first married, he would pop over for dinner, even though he knew what a terrible cook she was. Occasionally, he would appear for an evening the same way, unconsciously smoothing troubled waters between herself and Richard when he couldn't possibly know there *were* troubled waters; seemingly, he had come for a cup of coffee and conversation. Lorna had always thought he should have been spending his free evenings with an attractive blonde on his arm. Or brunette. Whatever his choice. All right, for some strange reason she and Matthew had always had a certain rapport, but that was before . . .

Before Richard had found her in a compromising position with another man. And it couldn't have been much more compromising, she reminded herself wearily as she set the cruise control and tried to relax for the trip home.

Eight and a half months after that episode, one blond baby had been born to two brunette parents. She had never cheated on Richard, but her word was not *fact,* and the Whitakers were sticklers for facts. Perhaps she could have fought the divorce, but the only *fact* she could have presented to any of them was a picture of herself as a child. A towhead, like Johnny, and like her mother and grandfather, all of whom had turned into brunettes as teenagers. So she could have produced a photograph, and she could even have subjected her baby to a paternity test, but Johnny's paternity was really only a moot point by then. She knew Richard had been looking for an excuse to divorce her. Faith, love, trust had all gone by the wayside; there was no marriage left to fight for by the time the child was born.

Richard was overly possessive and fiercely jealous—qualities that seemed to come with the male Whitaker genes. Richard, Sr., had at first treated her like a daughter . . . and later had treated her like scum. It was like turning over a record and finding on the flip side the ugly qualities in the men whom she had once cared for so much, whom she had trusted, who had trusted her...

She hadn't given Matthew the chance to hurt her as Richard and his father had. Matthew had tried to get her to talk; in retrospect, she could see that for a long time he had tried to help her through the turbulent marriage. Always kind, often there, perceptive, and calming... Richard had found it amusing that his formidable older brother had taken a little sister under his wing. But when push came to shove, Lorna had shut Matthew out. She was angry and frightened and young. Mr. Whitaker's contempt had hurt her to the core; contempt from Richard... Well, the end of the marriage had changed her whole life. To risk contempt from Matthew... it was too frightening, in some subtle way she never defined; she simply refused to lay herself open to it. It was easier just not to speak to him. Perhaps she knew unconsciously that there was some point at which she might completely break apart, splinter into a thousand little pieces...

And you wanted to get involved with him again?

Yes, she finally admitted wearily to herself. *Yes*. The marriage had scarred her, and badly. For many years, she hadn't had the energy or the desire to pursue a relationship with another man. Then, about two years ago, she had become aware not only that her son needed a father, but also that she had strong sexual and emotional needs that couldn't forever be sublimated in work and daydreams.

Fine. She'd discovered very quickly that most men really weren't all that eager to take on a woman *and* a half-grown son. Yet there were some. Enough so that at twenty-nine she was not particularly pleased to find herself turning into a tease. When a man came on too strong, all she could think of was that he might judge her easy, as Richard had judged her; that she was again putting herself into a position where she could be condemned without a trial, that she would be left vulnerable, without defenses...

She was *not* guilty. She was tired of *feeling* guilty. For Johnny's sake, and for her own, she wanted the truth spoken out loud, *t*'s crossed and *i*'s dotted.

So simple. So painfully simple. Yet Lorna's plans had gone haywire the moment Matthew had walked into his office. Matthew was not her brother-in-law anymore. He wasn't acting like a brother; she couldn't seem to *feel* that he was a brother...Leave it, she told herself. Serve him dinner and just try...

She pulled into the driveway of her apartment building, snatched up her purse, and opened the car door just as Matthew pulled up behind her. The biting wind whipped her coat open around her legs. "Turn up the thermostat out here, will you?" she shouted back to Matthew.

"I don't know what you're complaining about, Misha. You should be glad there are no mosquitoes." He pushed up the collar of his coat and dug his hands in his pockets as he followed her to the front door.

Why was she shivering now that they were inside? The tiny vestibule seemed crowded with the two of them hanging up their coats. Matthew's arm brushed hers, and she felt surrounded suddenly, by his arms that seemed to be everywhere, by the almost-familiar scent of his after shave, by the physical power that seemed to vibrate around him. Snow still glistened in his hair, and when she turned from the closet she had a sense of déjà vu as if she had once raked her fingers through his damp hair, though of course she hadn't. Their eyes met, but only for an instant.

When he looked away, Lorna wondered vaguely if she was coming down with the flu. Something was definitely wrong with her. Her pulse was beating out of control, and Matthew had the oddest look in his eyes...She stepped into the living room ahead of him. "Feel free to look around," she suggested lightly. "I just need a minute to brush my hair; then I'll get us both a drink."

He wasn't in the kitchen when she came out of the bathroom, for which she was grateful. Except for some wine and a little brandy, she didn't stock much liquor in the house, and had no desire to be caught standing on a chair fetching the wineglasses. She was just putting the chair back in place when he showed up in the doorway. "The place looks like you, Misha," he commented lazily. "Ten thousand plants and a dozen half-read books and all soft colors—"

"I don't understand it," Lorna admitted wryly. "When I look at a decorating magazine, I always love the spacious, serene stuff, yet my own house ends up thoroughly cluttered." She tried to twist the corkscrew into the dusty bottle she'd found in the bottom cupboard.

"I'll do that." His hands closed on her hips, and he shifted her so he could work at the counter; she stared at him, startled at the slight intimacy. He glanced at her with just the faintest hint of a smile. "You haven't gained any weight."

"A few pounds."

"Upstairs, then. There's nothing extra downstairs." He turned his attention to the wine bottle as she determinedly made a big business out of getting dinner ready, totally flustered by the comment. After Johnny was born, she had...developed. But Matthew had always been extremely proper in anything he'd ever said to her. She was surprised that he'd even noticed...

"You're even more beautiful than I remembered, Misha. And I find that hard to believe." He turned to offer her a glass of wine, his dark eyes expressive, yet unfathomable. "You were totally oblivious to it back then," he said quietly. "You didn't seem to know how beautiful you were. How special."

She took the glass and gulped down half of the wine. So much for composure and poise, she thought idly, and refused to look at him. Stop feeling unhinged, she told herself. "You've done well for yourself, Matthew. I kept expecting to read in the papers that you'd married." That sounded . . . wonderful. She gave herself a mental pat on the back. Cool, polite, proper conversation . . . She finished the wine, set the glass on the counter, and put the meat loaf back in the refrigerator.

"Wasn't that for dinner?"

"The refrigerator heats up faster than the oven," she said blandly.

"I see."

She regarded him with a brilliantly cheerful smile, daring him to make a single remark. But there was nothing. Just a wicked pair of dark eyes and another slash of a smile. She took the meat loaf out again and put it in the oven, tried to dredge up some pride for remembering to turn the dial on, and turned her attention to the potatoes. "We'll have to eat in here," she informed him. "I'm afraid the dining room's been converted to an office for me. With only two bedrooms, I had to have a place to work."

"I saw the foreign dictionaries."

It took her a moment to figure out why he was rummaging in her refrigerator, until he removed fresh vegetables and lined them up on the counter. Ah, yes, salad. "Matthew, you don't have to do that—"

He paid no attention. "So you're working as a translator?"

She nodded, trying not to smile. He had bent down in front of a cupboard and was reaching across the peanut butter to get to the bowls, almost tipping over the flour on the way.

"I had only one skill to sell in the job market when

Johnny was a baby," she explained. "I was fluent in French and Russian because my parents spoke those languages. And I had studied German in school... Well, you know that, Matthew, but I still didn't have a degree. I started tutoring, and then an electronics firm in Detroit decided to try reaching the European market and I translated some brochures for them. My clientele built up, slowly but surely; Dad helped for a long time. I do a good deal of work for four travel companies, but computer manufacturers are really becoming my bread and butter; there seems to be no end to the software that's being peddled overseas..."

Why are you chattering on? she thought. He doesn't want to hear all that. She fell silent, first putting the potatoes in the oven and then rapidly cleaning the counter before setting the table. Matthew was busy shredding lettuce, the sleeves of his starched white shirt now rolled up. "Didn't your father have life insurance, Misha?"

She nodded. "But I used it to pay his medical bills. I've managed," she said, with a small trace of defiance. "I've done fine, Matthew. I make a decent living, and the work allows me to be home with Johnny. It's just... it simply hasn't been possible for me to save a great deal of money, and the tuition for this special school for Johnny—"

"I already said you could have the money, Misha. You don't need to justify its use to me." His voice was quiet but held a trace of steel in it. He didn't want to hear or talk about Johnny. He leaned back against the counter, drinking his wine while Lorna finished setting the table. "Between caring for your father and a small child and working, you couldn't have had much time for a social life."

She felt a prickle at the back of her neck and glanced up. He was staring at her with brooding dark eyes, his look so possessive that it took her aback. "I can guarantee you've had a more active social life than I have over the years," Lorna said lightly, but there was steel in her voice, too. If he was trying to imply that she had little chance to be promiscuous...

"No, Misha..."

Gently, his palm brushed her cheek, but whatever he had been about to say was interrupted by four feet two inches of energetic towhead slamming through the back door. "Hi, mom!" Johnny offered her a token peck on the cheek, in between kicking off his boots, chewing on a thumbnail, hanging his coat on a hook, and never taking his eyes off the stranger for a second. "What's for dinner?"

"Meat loaf, sweets. Were you good for Freda?"

Johnny made a face. "A perfect angel. Par for the course."

Lorna smiled, but all she could think was: *Be* an angel, Johnny. Just this once. She turned to Matthew to make the introductions.

He was finishing the last of his wine in one long gulp, and when he set down his glass his dark gaze captured hers. His shoulders were stiff and his jaw firm. And his eyes were like black ice, their depths unfathomable but the chill unmistakable. Until that moment, Lorna had almost—foolishly, she rebuked herself—managed to believe that Matthew had put the past behind them.

She turned back to Johnny. Her son, unfortunately, didn't miss a trick. He stepped forward as he had been taught, offering a distinctly grubby hand as he knew he was required to do, but his normally soft gray eyes were wary, his shoulders stiff, and his little jaw as firm as Matthew's. Whitaker to the core, Lorna thought despairingly.

It was going to be one hell of a dinner.

CHAPTER
Three

LORNA REACHED OVER to tuck Johnny in, automatically straightening her son's cowlick as she bent to kiss him good night. "Don't stay up late," he ordered her sleepily.

Lorna smiled, flicking out the light next to him. "Sleep well, sweets. I love you."

"Mom."

She turned at the door.

"Where'd he come from? You never had him around before."

"Johnny," she said patiently, "I explained. He was someone I knew a long time ago; that was the reason I invited him for dinner."

"Yeah, I know what you said." Johnny hesitated, mashing back the pillow behind his head. "And he's okay. He's got a neat car, and all those stories about criminals and stuff. I mean, I like him fine, but I don't know about you. He's a man's man, you know?"

She swallowed a grin. "No, I'm not sure that I do."

"You just tell him to go home. You're tired."

And that was the truth, she thought as she detoured

into the bathroom before facing Matthew again. She brushed her hair into a thick glossy curtain that just touched her shoulders, then sat down on the edge of the porcelain tub and simply breathed. For the first time in hours.

So many conflicting emotions were churning inside her that she felt as though her heart had been put through a blender. It wasn't that the dinner had been so traumatic; it hadn't been. Johnny had gregariously taken over the conversation, and once he'd discovered that Matthew was a criminal lawyer, he'd grilled the attorney with all his nine-year-old's guile. No amount of softspoken admonishments or maternal kicks under the table had stopped his offensive. Johnny, the spoiled brat, considered it his right to vet any man Lorna saw. His hostility toward and mistrust of Matthew had been instant. The thaw had been marginal.

And Matthew, contrary to what she had expected, had fielded Johnny's every question and totally ignored her. He took the child's interrogation seriously and treated him with respect. A stranger might have even thought Matthew relaxed. But Lorna was vibrantly aware of the way the muscle in his jaw continually tightened, of the way he deliberately avoided looking at her, of the absolutely controlled quality of his voice. And when Johnny neatly sidestepped helping with the dishes and ignored Lorna's request to pick up his toys, Matthew's black eyes had fired, though he hadn't said a word.

It was hardly an instant love affair between uncle and nephew. Not that Lorna had expected it to be, but she hadn't anticipated how it would wrench her heart to see the two of them together. Both hoarded their feelings as if they were gold; both had the same square jaw; both were possessive and protective. Johnny's right shoulder shifted exactly the way Matthew's did when he was uncomfortable. They had beautiful, even white teeth. Both had an abundance of arrogant self-confidence, a quality Lorna alternately resented and envied.

Tears threatened suddenly. Matthew was family. He and Richard, Sr., were the only family Johnny had besides her. She stood up, rapidly applying a bit of blusher to her cheeks. She hadn't been this emotionally exhausted in a long time, and she had no desire to face Matthew again. She knew he hadn't seen beyond Johnny's blond hair and freckles. The only conclusion she could possibly draw was that Johnny reminded him of the kind of woman he thought she was or had been. The kind of woman who would be unfaithful less than a year into her marriage, the kind for whom a vow of love meant so little . . .

Lorna slipped off her high-heeled shoes, irrationally deciding that she could face anything as long as her toes weren't pinched, and padded back out into the living room.

Matthew was standing before the white marble fireplace, looking at a photograph of Lorna and Johnny at a picnic a few years before. His glass of brandy was next to him on the mantel; another glass was waiting for her on the coffee table. He turned to look at her as she entered the room; the reserved smile he'd managed for Johnny was gone, replaced by an expression of authority and determination. As she gazed at his stern features and dark, impenetrable eyes, Lorna felt distinctly uneasy.

She bent to pick up her glass and then sat down in a corduroy armchair, curling one leg beneath her.

"Shall we get the details out of the way, Misha? Exactly when do you need the money?" he asked flatly.

She hesitated. "I don't need the whole ten thousand dollars, Matthew," she said quietly. "Only enough to pay Johnny's tuition for this year. Johnny *needs* this school, but my furnace went out last week, which is why I started to panic—"

"The question was only *when*, Misha, not how much."

She took a sip of brandy and let it flow down her throat before answering. He was standing with his feet apart and one elbow resting on the mantel; the stance was aggressive, all authoritative male, and she thought, No, Matthew, I'll be damned if I'm going to let myself get defensive. Not for anyone, not anymore. Her tone was low and very, very controlled. "The school he's in has all but asked me to find another place for him. Johnny's bright, Matthew. Too bright. When he gets ahead of the others, he's bored . . . but any kid who calls him 'brain' gets a punch in the nose. He's already played hookey several times. Of course, he only goes to the library, but—"

"Misha, I don't have to hear all about the boy's problems. The only thing I really need to know is when you want the money."

Her smoky eyes darkened expressively as she set down her glass. She didn't care if Matthew could read the signs of impending anger: She flicked her hair back; her chin stiffened; her eyes took on the ominous gray of a stormcloud. "Next week," she clipped out.

Matthew finished his drink and leaned back against the marble fireplace, loosely folding his arms. "Honey. Stop bristling."

"Look—"

"For you, Misha, I'd do my best to walk on water. When I saw you again and realized you were in trouble . . ." He shook his head, just a little, his eyes holding hers in a gaze so intense she could not look away. She wanted to. Something kept happening whenever he looked at her, whenever he was close enough to touch her—something completely different from the way she had once felt about Matthew. "You're unhappy because I don't want to listen to you talk about your son," he said quietly. "At least let me explain, Misha. I don't feel I have the right—not to even offer you a few words of advice, not even simply to listen. His own father surely has first rights. Stone's still living in the city. Even though things apparently didn't work out between you, he has the financial and moral responsibility to take care of Johnny's needs. Why don't you go to him first, Misha?"

She looked away then, every nerve ending coiling up tight. *"Never* would I go to that man. First of all, because he's a bastard. And second, because Johnny isn't. He's a Whitaker, Matthew . . ."

"And I never thought we had a problem with honesty," Matthew responded coldly. "Misha, he's your son. That's all that matters."

"Not to me!" She sprang from the chair and stalked to the closet to get his coat. Two huge tears that she had no intention of shedding stung her eyes. With Matthew's coat in her arms, Lorna turned back to him; her silvery eyes were brilliant in her pale face. "Not to me, Matthew," she repeated more calmly. "You're just like Richard. Just like your father. Do you think I would sleep with two men at the same time? Do you think I would put a ring on my finger and then, less than a year later—"

"Misha—"

"It was fun, being a nymphomaniac," she said bitterly. "It was a short-term illness, but it was wonderful while it lasted. Just anyone who asked me . . . ah, well, those certainly were the good old days. And it was certainly wonderful seeing you again, Matthew. As in good night."

He hadn't moved. She could see the coal-black sheen of his eyes from clear across the room. Then he started moving forward, slowly and deliberately. She could almost feel the tautness of his control, yet his voice sounded low. Velvet low. "You were a beautiful lady, Misha. I never saw you as anything other than a beautiful, sensitive, very special lady. Very, very young. Butterfly shy, easily frightened..." He was very close now, and she caught her breath as she realized he was reaching out for her.

"No." The word almost inaudible.

"Lonely..."

"Matthew—"

His fingers started, very gently, to thread through her hair. His thumb idly caressed the tender line of her jaw, raising her face to his. Through a blur of tears, she could see the smoldering passion in his charcoal eyes. "You were a girl then. Not nearly as beautiful as you are now. I wanted to protect you like an older brother when I saw things going so wrong. Don't think I would have touched you then, Misha, because I never would have. Never," he echoed.

Yet he did now. His lips gently met hers, soft, teasing, giving the briefest taste of him, hinting evocatively at the passion he was holding back. His huge palms cradled her face, and tenderly he brushed away the moisture beneath her eyes. Move away, Lorna, she told herself, but somehow she couldn't obey that inner command. Nothing made sense. A sudden rush of disturbing emotions whispered through her, sensual feelings that couldn't possibly belong to her. She'd never wanted Matthew. He'd never wanted her. Yet something crazy in his voice, that low, hypnotic, velvet voice of his, stirred up yearnings and desires and promises, the most irresistible of promises...

"So beautiful," he murmured. "I've missed you, Misha. Not the girl you were, but the woman you are. Can you understand that? It has nothing to do with another place and time. It has to do with now, the way you smile. The look in your eyes, Misha, the

way you flare up, the way you vibrate with emotion..."

His coat was between them; then suddenly wasn't.
Ever so slowly his mouth captured hers again, but
this time he didn't release her. His lips lingered, increasing their pressure as his arms enfolded her; her
senses reeled, and she was helpless under the assault
of textures and scents and sounds that were uniquely
Matthew. He liked his shirts starched; she knew no
other man who wore starched shirts anymore. The
fabric was slightly abrasive against the soft flesh of
her palm, its stiffness a denial of the warm, mobile
muscle and flesh of his shoulders. The collar had no
give to it at all; she felt she had won a battle when
her fingers finally reached the yielding flesh of his
neck, so vital, like Matthew, so electrifyingly virile,
like Matthew. His hair curled around her fingers, thick
and silky. Everything—the soap he used; the after
shave he splashed on; the shampoo he favored...they
were all Matthew. Not Richard. Not any other man.
And suddenly, neither past nor future existed.

With increasing hunger, his mouth covered hers;
his tongue dipped inside, and they shared the intimate
taste of each other. One of his hands cradled her head,
and the other stroked down her neck and her back to
the base of her spine, urging her closer to him. She
felt a crazy series of shivers run through her body, as
if every nerve ending had suddenly responded to this
unique man, to what he was feeling, to what he needed,
to what he wanted.

His mouth captured hers with such intensity that
she could sense his own conflicting emotions. He had
not come here for this—she knew it; he had not intended to touch her...yet he didn't stop. His hands
tattooed desperate, almost savage messages into her
flesh as he kneaded it through the soft knit dress, firing

the same explosive feelings in her. It was all wrong
. . . and so impossibly right. Never had she imagined
such sweet, fierce hunger as she now felt.

He wrapped his arms tightly around her, as if he
could lock her to him, mold her body to his. His heart
was pounding against hers, between her aching breasts,
pounding so hard she could feel his urgency, his desire. The hard pressure against her stomach and the
thrust and parry of his tongue inside her mouth con-
veyed a fierce need that was getting out of their control, but she didn't care. She didn't care . . .

"Oh, Matthew . . ."

"Hush, Misha. I'm not going to hurt you. I'm
not . . . just let me hold you." His evening beard grazed
her cheek as his lips nuzzled her throat. "Just let me
hold you," he repeated more softly. He cradled her
head, urging her cheek to his shoulder, and his lips
pressed into her hair. Her arms circling his waist, she
closed her eyes, feeling very close to tears.

If subconsciously she had felt this way about Matthew before, she'd had no inkling of it. He had always
been strong and protective and gentle with her, but
she had never conceived of him as anything but a
friend; she'd never have believed that she could want
Matthew so badly, that wanting could feel a need to
inhale him the way her lungs needed to inhale oxygen.
Richard had nothing to do with it. It was Matthew,
pure and simple. Only it was far from simple.

She hadn't forgotten Johnny. She hadn't forgotten
that Matthew still believed Johnny was conceived in
adultery . . . and it mattered, desperately, but not now.
Now, it seemed like a century since anyone had held
her.

"Misha . . ."

Reluctantly, he was trying to put space between
them, and her arms tightened as she raised her face
to his. "No," she whispered fiercely. *Don't move away,*

her heart cried. She knew all the reasons why they shouldn't be doing this. She had been cautious and careful for years, backing out of every relationship long before she risked getting hurt. She knew better than to take such a risk with Matthew; she was conscious that he had the capacity to hurt her. It didn't make sense. "Just for a minute," she murmured.

His answer was a ghost of a smile as his lips descended on hers again, this time courting her pleasure with tenderness. With a lazy, slow movement, his palms traced the shape of her, molding, exploring her hips and then her waist. One hand slid up to cradle the orb of her breast, then trailed higher to simply caress the soft skin of her throat. Simply? The hollow in her throat suddenly felt as soft as satin, as fragile as a rose petal, as sensitive as the pulse that beat so erratically within it. His lips tasted, savored, promised, deliberately coveting her response, taking pleasure from it. "Always so loving, Misha," he murmured. "So much love in you. So sweet..."

He slid the back zipper of her dress halfway down, then pushed the material aside, baring her neck and shoulders. He kissed the hollow above her collarbone, his lips so smooth and warm on that sensitive skin that a shudder rose from deep inside her. His tender mastery stirred sensual yearnings so strong that all her blood seemed to rush to her head. She felt dizzy, lightheaded, feverish. She couldn't seem to keep her hands still, wanting to touch him, wanting to explore his skin. "Misha," he murmured, "you know damn well what you're asking for..."

Yes. Him. Matthew. An hour with him, a day. She felt richer where he touched; her skin felt cherished; she felt a freedom to touch and explore that she had never felt before, a need to please and to know... Her lips clung to his, groping to tell him. It was not just sex, but she didn't know what it was. She was a little frightened and very, very high, and she drank in his warmth, her hands roaming his back.

His breathing was harsh and labored. "God, I want you," he groaned. He unzipped her dress completely, and his hands stole inside, kneading the flesh of her back, making sensual circular motions on her thin silk slip . . .

"Just what do you think you're doing to my mother?"

An electric volt shot through Lorna as she heard the belligerent voice of her son. Matthew stiffened, and they both jerked around to face Johnny, who was standing in the doorway to the hall.

"I wasn't hurting your mother, Johnny," Matthew immediately assured the boy. Lorna could not believe how calm his voice sounded. Her throat was dry and her fingers trembling, her body not at all prepared to cope with the abrupt withdrawal of Matthew's touch.

"It sure looked to me like you were." Johnny's sleep-laden eyes were nevertheless furious; his chin jutted forward with all the aggression of a man twice his size. "Nobody hurts my mother, mister. You better just get out of here."

"Johnny!" The child had his fists clenched as if ready to take on the grown man. A year later, she might remember that instant and smile; but at this precise instant she was afraid of what would happen. "He was *not* hurting me. Honey, go back to bed—"

"Mom, don't *lie*. I can take care of him—"

If she had been looking at Matthew, she might have seen a half-smile on his lips. But she was looking at her son, groping for the proper words. Her maternal instincts had never failed her before; but now she stood as if paralyzed. Her flesh was still warm from Matthew's touch, her heart still beating wildly. She shivered violently as Matthew zipped her dress up and rested a quietly supportive hand on her shoulder.

"Johnny, I would never hurt your mother," Mat-

thew assured him quietly. "You have every right to
be concerned about anyone who might. I'll be leaving
the house within the next five minutes. You can keep
your door open when you go back to bed."

There was a silence. "Well..." Johnny's fists slowly
unclenched, but he aimed a look of total distrust at
Matthew.

"Matthew wasn't hurting me, honey," Lorna
echoed, and took a long breath.

Johnny wasn't looking at her. "You're leaving
soon?" he insisted to Matthew.

"I'm leaving soon," Matthew agreed.

The child stalked back through the dark hallway.
When Lorna turned around again, Matthew was bending over to pick up his coat, but his eyes met hers.
A twinkle of something dark and private passed between them. "That's quite a chaperon you have there.
It's pretty impossible to believe he'd take it kindly if
he woke up one morning to find someone in bed next
to you."

"Well, of course, I wouldn't..." Her first impulse
was to defend herself. Of course she wouldn't allow
some strange man in bed with her while her half-
grown son was asleep in the next room! But she didn't
finish the sentence, aware from the way Matthew's
eyes pierced hers that he'd already come to that conclusion. A conclusion, she thought fleetingly, that
should be none of his business.

He adjusted his collar, buttoned his suit jacket, and
reached for the overcoat he had tossed on a chair.
Suddenly, he was all control and authority again; he
faced her as Matthew Whitaker, the imposing attorney, and she could no longer read any emotion in his
dark eyes. "Misha, whatever you're thinking, I didn't
come here to seduce you. That had nothing to do with
my brother, with your boy. If you're angry..."

She sucked in her breath, feeling shaky inside.

"No." But she was frightened by the feelings he'd evoked in her. Because all the same, his brother and her child made even the simplest touch between her and Matthew far too complicated. She looked away from him and crossed her arms as she followed him to the door.

He opened it, letting in a sudden chill and the glow of moonlight on snow-covered street. The night had turned silent; the afternoon snowstorm had worn itself out, and the wind had abated. He looked out and then turned back, raising his hand to her cheek. She curled her face into his palm, aching inside, as her eyes searched his. "I don't see how it can possibly work, Misha."

She nodded, unable to deny it.

"My father and your son are involved, and they've already been hurt."

She knew it all. And worse, she knew also that Matthew still believed she had been unfaithful to Richard. The trust so vital to any kind of meaningful relationship could never be there for him.

"Do you want me to call you?" he asked quietly.

No, said her every instinct of self-preservation. But she nodded, and he turned to go out into the black, still night.

Lorna had checked on the sleeping Johnny, turned off the lights, and locked the door, and was now immersed to the shoulders in a steaming hot bath, her eyes closed and a towel wrapped around her head like a turban. She thought of Matthew, and then she thought of her son, and then she thought of Matthew . . . but finally, almost inevitably, her thoughts settled on Richard's friend and mentor, Ron Stone.

She'd fallen in love with Richard when he was studying for the bar—terrible timing, any attorney would have told her, but then, Lorna had grown up in an academic atmosphere. Richard was immersed in law books seven days a week, but when he did come up for air they were together...They seemed to live on fast food and late-night conversations after the rest of the world had long been asleep, the two of them isolated in a very private world. Richard was her first love, her only lover; within a week after he at last passed the bar, he put a wedding ring on her finger, and their life was abruptly turned upside down.

Ron Stone was older than her husband by ten years. He was tall and blond, as Ivy League as alligator shirts, as smooth as whipped cream, and as good-looking as a tennis pro. An attorney, naturally. Divorce was his specialty, although he didn't seem to favor divorcées. He liked young, beautiful, and unforgivably stupid married women.

He liked Lorna.

Richard had turned into a stranger the day he was admitted to the bar. He worked for the law firm sixty, sometimes seventy hours a week; at night he and a reluctant Lorna partied with a fast-moving crowd, some of whom swapped mates to keep from being bored. Ron Stone headed that pack. Lorna considered him a vulture, but Richard thought him an irreplaceable key that would unlock the doors Richard wished to enter. Ron Stone knew all the right people, could help Richard make all the right contacts. Coming from a successful family, Richard wanted to make his own name in his own way, and *now*. If that meant using people...well, Ron Stone was a master at that game. From the first he took on Lorna as his own personal little cause. There was no talking to Richard about Stone's lifestyle or her uneasiness at his innuendos, especially since his behavior to her was impeccable whenever Richard was within sight.

Her husband would change back to the man she'd fallen in love with, Lorna told herself a thousand times; all he needed was a little confidence under his belt, some successes he could call his own. Any new marriage requires adjustments, and she desperately wanted her marriage to be successful . . . but it wasn't. Critical, jealous, possessive, domineering . . . Richard had not shown any of these traits before they were married, but now he had them all in abundance. She couldn't even try to talk with him. And Ron Stone kept coming on to her.

He cornered her at every party. Every social gathering. He started calling her at home. Nothing she said or did put him off, and it got to the point where she wasn't sleeping nights and was afraid to stay home during the day. She became nervous around Richard, telling white lies to explain why she wasn't home when he called. They fought. He was trying so hard to do well; he wanted so much for both of them . . . but Lorna was lonely and frightened and floundering. She couldn't simply tell Ron Stone to shove it, because Richard thought so much of him; she didn't tell Richard about Ron, because she was afraid he wouldn't believe her, because she didn't want to seem naive, because she thought she should be able to handle it . . . She had a dozen reasons. And then one day Ron had evidently decided he was tired of the hunt and chase; Lorna was home in bed with a cold the day he moved in for the kill. A half-hour after he arrived, Richard raced in unexpectedly to pick up a brief he'd forgotten. He found his wife just inside the front door dressed in a filmy nightgown, in what must have looked very much like a parting embrace after a morning tryst with a verbally creative Ron Stone . . .

End of story, Lorna thought wryly, and flicked open the drain. She stood up, wrapping a towel around herself as she stepped out of the tub. That single afternoon had caused such endless heartache when the solution had really been so simple: Buy an eight-gauge shotgun, the kind once used on elephants, and murder one Ron Stone.

She rubbed a towel over the mirror to wipe off the steam, and saw a pair of haunted gray eyes looking back at her. Ron Stone was not really to blame. She knew that. He was just a predator in a world of predators.

Guilt had haunted her for a long time. She was guilty of not telling Richard; she was guilty of walking a tightrope with Ron when she should have dealt honestly with the situation from the outset. Those were petty guilts, next to the real one—her guilt over a marriage gone wrong...

Lorna turned off the bathroom light, padded barefoot to her bedroom, and slipped on a nightgown in the darkness. In just seconds, her head was on the pillow, but her eyes still blinked wide open in the night. That episode of her life was like a door that wouldn't close, a bad dream that just refused to end. Richard hadn't believed her version of the incident— her *true* version—but he had tried to save the marriage. He rather had to; two weeks later, the pregnancy test came out positive. The next eight months were a nightmare; they both tried and failed. There was just no trust left to build on. No love. And the day Johnny was born, blond like Ron, about eight and a half months after that terrible morning...

Richard had been killed in a car accident when Johnny was a year and a half old. The divorce was final by then, but Matthew had sent a note to tell her of his brother's death. During the divorce proceedings, Matthew had tried a dozen times to talk with her, but she'd shut him off every time. Perhaps she didn't really want to tell him the story because in her heart she already knew there was no point in trying to salvage the marriage. Perhaps she didn't want to tell him because, from the first time she met him, she knew she occupied a special, if tiny, niche in his life, and that mattered to her. She'd had his respect, his gentle teasing, his supportive caring... and now she was so ashamed.

It had taken her a long time to put her life back together. She had regained her self-respect, earned her independence. Self-sufficiency was her goal; and she achieved it. The toughest hurdle had been regaining her lost pride. Lorna vowed never again to let anyone get into a position to judge her without a trial; and love without trust... could never be love. She had been overwhelmed by bitterness against Richard—and his father—for judging her... She was not likely to forget the experience.

And Matthew was a Whitaker as well. She hadn't forgotten that either. But Johnny had a right to know his father's family... His isolation from the Whitakers had bothered her for a long time. Her son had a right to his last name, a right to the financial support the Whitakers could give him.

Fine, Lorna, she told herself in the darkness. Fine.

If Matthew had ever felt anything other than brotherly love for her, she hadn't known it. She certainly hadn't had any sexual feelings toward him. Matthew was terrifying; a successful, formidable, too-quiet man whom she had once taken ridiculous pleasure in getting to laugh. She knew he'd honestly wanted her marriage to succeed. He had never so much as laid his little finger on her in a sexual way...

So what happened today? she asked herself. She closed her eyes in the darkness. How on earth had it all happened? How had they ended up touching... kissing... Matthew's last name alone should have precluded the kind of feelings Lorna had experienced tonight. The name Whitaker meant pain to Lorna. No trust. Men hung up on black-and-white truths, possessive, judgmental...

She'd been a fool to tell him he could call, Lorna decided wearily. She had only opened the door to more heartache. She'd just feel she was on trial all over again; there'd never be any trust. She'd never again sacrifice trust in a relationship, and she had to think of Johnny.

She did, right before sleep finally overcame her.

CHAPTER
Four

"JOHNNY, YOU'VE GOT two choices," Lorna called out, tapping her booted foot impatiently. "Either get the lead out of your feet or get grounded for the next ninety-seven years."

The rapid pounding of boots was eventually followed by the entrance of her grinning son. "I don't know why you bother to threaten me," he said cheekily, pecking her affectionately on the chin as he headed outside ahead of her. "You know you aren't really going to really do anything. Besides, we're an hour earlier than you said."

"Three-quarters of an hour now," Lorna scolded as she hurried toward her Camaro.

"I told you school was going okay."

"And I told you I wanted to see for myself," she replied, turning the key in the ignition.

"You'll be bored. It's just for kids." He paused and gave her a sidelong look. "Come to think of it, you'll probably fit right in."

"Thanks, urchin."

The forty-minute drive to Johnny's new private

school took all of Lorna's concentration; they stopped talking. A fresh layer of snow had fallen overnight, hiding an equally fresh layer of ice. Her car liked to skid, and the roads were giving it every opportunity.

Just less than an hour later the two walked down the silent corridors of the school. Not another soul was in sight at seven-thirty, but a beacon of light emanated from the farthest doorway. Johnny had been here only two weeks, yet each day Lorna had to fight with herself not to worry about how he was adjusting, not to show anxiety to her son, not to come on like an overprotective mother. When Mrs. Wright had called the night before, inviting Lorna to see how Johnny was functioning in the classroom, it was all Lorna could do to force herself to go to bed rather than pace the floor all night.

"Mrs. Whitaker?" The young blond woman smiled, rising from a clutter of papers on the carpet when she saw Lorna and Johnny. "You two are early birds." While Johnny was hanging up his coat, the teacher said simply, "I realize that you visited the classroom before you enrolled your son here. But I know Johnny a little better now, so I thought at this point I could give you a definite idea what we want to do together."

Lorna nodded. "He's doing all right?"

"He's doing fine."

The look of the classroom still surprised Lorna. Bright print curtains hung at the windows; carpeting warmed the floor; there was no blackboard. The school practiced Montessori methods, which meant that each student had an individually structured program based on his interests and abilities, regardless of his age. Under the teacher's supervision, each student was allowed to work at his own pace; it had seemed ideal for an exceptional child like Johnny, and yet Lorna was concerned about discipline and socialization.

Certainly she had never seen a better-equipped

classroom. A fourth-grader with a gift for languages was able to choose not only from among all the modern and even classical languages, but hieroglyphics as well. Geography included not only globes and standard texts, but also clay and water, materials with which the children constructed their own topographical maps. Two computers offered math challenges up to college-level statistics. All the materials and supplies were of high quality, plentiful, and visually appealing.

The school was expensive far beyond what Lorna could have afforded had she not gone to Matthew, but it was the only school that suited Johnny's unique abilities and personality. In public school, instead of taking pride in his quick mind, he had felt like an outcast when he mastered new skills and concepts more rapidly than his classmates.

". . . lazy with his reading," Mrs. Wright was saying. "Oh, I know he's well ahead of grade level, but as I told you, that isn't the point. He could be working up to his potential more, but we'll just take care of that without his knowing." Mrs. Wright winked conspiratorily. "I didn't see him objecting when I put a seventh-grade science text in front of him yesterday. I think he was expecting an extended Dick-and-Jane basal reader."

"But is he making friends? Does he seem to be adjusting? Academic achievement is important to me, Mrs. Wright, but . . ."

"But it's not everything." The teacher nodded her curly blond head, and then hesitated. "Johnny seems to like the other children, but he is a bit sensitive, isn't he? I don't want to pry, but I understand his father is no longer alive—"

Lorna cast a haunted look toward her son, who was working away at the far end of the room. "Actually, we were divorced before Richard died." She took a breath. "It doesn't help that I'm estranged from my former husband's family as well. Johnny knows all of that. Actually, he seemed to accept the situation very well, perhaps because I told him about it when he was younger. Now...I know there are questions in his mind that he just hasn't asked yet. Maybe he's afraid to ask. And I..."

"Mrs. Whitaker..." The teacher gently touched her hand. "Johnny is fine. Many children these days don't have large families. For that matter, there are increasing numbers of children in single-parent households. It doesn't mean he won't grow up to be a well-adjusted man—"

Yes, Lorna reassured herself as she walked back out to the car a few minutes later. She started the engine feeling more lighthearted than she had in months. Johnny had not been an easy child to raise. In her own elementary school days, she'd excelled in the first two of the three *R*'s but arithmetic had always been her Waterloo, and in high school she'd never had a prayer of passing chemistry, while algebra might as well have been Arabic. No, she wasn't a dunce, but she certainly hadn't had Johnny's insatiable intellectual curiosity; at times just trying to keep one step ahead of him was exhausting. At least the teachers at this school seemed to understand her son...

Matthew, she thought as she drove home, I owe you. Believing Johnny had the right to that tuition money because of his Whitaker bloodline was one thing, but Matthew *didn't* believe that, and yet he had given without question or catch...

Once at home, she opened the door, set down her purse, and was just hanging up her coat when the phone rang.

"Come over for coffee," Freda croaked into the

receiver. "Although actually, I'm having tea."

"You're home from work with a cold?" Lorna guessed.

"I never get colds. I'm playing hookey for the day," Freda croaked. "And bring aspirin."

Armed with aspirin, cold pills, cough medicine, and a thermos of chamomile tea, Lorna walked the twenty steps to her neighbor's apartment and let herself in. "Freda!"

"In here."

"I can only stay a minute; I've got a ton of work to do today." Lorna shed her coat and tossed it on the only empty chair in the living room. Toys, clothes, magazines, and needlework took up the rest of the space. Freda always made Lorna feel like a model housekeeper. A smile playing at the corners of her lips, she wended her way through the chaos to the kitchen.

Red-nosed and sniffling, Freda was bundled up in a bathrobe with her feet propped up on a kitchen chair.

"Tell Brian to come over tonight after school," Lorna ordered promptly, moving swiftly to line up the medicines on the table.

"I'll be completely recovered by this afternoon," Freda rasped.

"You look like something the cat rejected." Familiar with Freda's kitchen, Lorna reached for a second cup in the cupboard, filled it with instant coffee and water, and set it in the microwave.

"I *always* look like hell when you walk in the room. God knows why I even associate with a single female who looks the way you do. Masochism. Why don't you dye your hair gray and gain forty pounds?"

Grinning, Lorna retrieved her cup of coffee, set it on the counter, and ran a sinkful of soapy water. "Every time you talk, you breathe. If you give me that cold, Freda, I'm going to boil you in oil, so just sit back and drink your tea."

"I didn't ask you over to wash my dishes!"

Lorna paid no attention, adding the dirty dishes to the hot, sudsy water. Freda would have done the same for her if she were ill. The friendship was two years old and thriving. Lorna watched both boys after school until Freda came home from work; in return Freda baby-sat whenever Lorna wanted to go out for the evening. It was so easy, living next to each other; the boys even liked each other. Freda was a bitter divorcée, abandoned by her ex for a younger woman. Lorna had heard the story a hundred times; by nature compassionate, she would gladly listen to it another hundred times, or however often it took for Freda to get the residue out of her system.

Finishing the dishes, she turned to wipe her hands on a towel and found Freda staring bleary-eyed at her, a peculiar expression on her face. "What's wrong?" She frowned absently. "You want me to throw a wash in the machine?"

"I want you to sit down for a minute," Freda commanded hoarsely.

"I will. For a minute. But I've got a rush job I really have to finish today..." Lorna darted back to the bedrooms and returned a moment later with an armful of clothes. "What is it about boys? An allergy to clothes hampers that comes with the Y chromosome? Whenever I want to do laundry, the first place I look is under Johnny's bed—"

"*Sit.*"

"I *will.*" Once the wash was started, Lorna blew back a strand of hair from her cheek, took her coffee cup to the far side of Freda's table, and settled down with a sigh. "You want your tea heated up?"

Freda sneezed and grabbed for the box of tissues.

"What I *want* is to know if you're still planning to go out with that man tomorrow night."

Lorna took a sip of coffee, averting her eyes. "Obviously not, if you're still sick."

"Don't be an idiot, Lorna Whitaker! The boys could care less if I've got a cold when they're sleeping. That's not why I asked. Honey, I don't think you've really thought this out."

"I've done nothing *but* think it out," Lorna responded, with conscious control.

"And how did you explain Matthew to Johnny? The same last name and all that?"

"I haven't explained."

Freda gave her a pointed look and continued the attack. Gently, for Freda. "Honey, I'm just afraid you're going to get hurt. What's to be gained by your seeing anyone in that family again? You actually think he's looking to be a father to Johnny after what happened with his brother? That you can both just forget what happened?"

Lorna stirred her coffee, making obsessive circles over and over. "I don't know," she admitted finally. She looked at Freda with an open, honest countenance. "I don't seem to know . . . anything. Matthew has called at least twice a week for the last few weeks— and I've found myself laughing. No man has made me laugh for ages . . . Matthew always used to be able to make me laugh. We just keep . . . talking. And I tell myself that if I continue to see him, in time he'll believe me about Johnny. In time, he might even see for himself the Whitaker characteristics I see in Johnny—"

"Lorna."

Freda could ferret out fibs like a fox. Lorna rolled her eyes and sighed, but she wasn't smiling. "All right." She shrugged. "The laughter does matter—

desperately—to me. But it isn't all that happens when
he calls. When I hear his voice. It's as if we've both
found each other, found someone to talk to, someone
who seems to understand all those things you don't
know how to say. Part of that closeness was there
before, I can see that now, but Richard aside, a relationship between Matthew and me wouldn't have
worked then. Matthew was a man and he was just
being kind to a frightened girl in those days. But
now..."

"And it never occurred to you that he might be out
to take you for a ride, Lorna?" Freda demanded. "You
think he's forgotten his brother? He still believes you
cheated on Richard..."

Lorna's smile died. She got up to take her empty
cup to the counter. "I don't know," she said again.
"Or maybe I do, a little. Matthew's not motivated by
revenge, if that's what you're trying to say, Freda.
He's too sensitive, too fair; he knew at the time that
there were two sides to the story and that Richard
wasn't perfect. He was good to his brother, but they
weren't...close. He isn't...pursuing me because of
that. Sex might be another story."

Freda sneezed. "Pardon?"

"Sex," Lorna repeated clearly.

Freda's eyebrows shot up in alarm. "Has a stranger
just walked into this kitchen?"

"I'm just trying very hard to be honest with myself—"

"Honey, for two years I've been urging you to give
free rein to your libido. But not with this man. You
can't build a relationship on sexual attraction alone,
kiddo. You'll get broken up into little pieces if that
man uses you."

Lorna shook her head and headed for the door, her
eyes suddenly distant. "Only one man ever used me,

Freda, and no one else is ever going to do it again.
For now, not to worry. Pour yourself another cup of
tea and crawl into bed."

Lorna, wearing a pale coral slip, was riffling through
her closet with a look of dissatisfaction. She worked
at home and didn't have to dress for success; conse-
quently, her wardrobe was decidedly limited. So was
her decision-making ability this evening. Everything
was wrong. The raspberry shirtwaist was too bright.
The coral print too busy. The mauve too dull. All the
shirtwaists were boring. The suit she'd thought she
loved she now hated . . . Her fingers touched the softness of an angora skirt and hesitated.

A few moments later, she'd exchanged the coral
slip for a black one, pulled on a scooped-neck black
cashmere sweater, and was stepping into the angora
skirt, which had a bold black, gray, and purple patch-
work pattern. She'd made the skirt a year ago. The
project had been fun. The dramatic colors appealed
to her, and the angora added substance to her slim
hips. So why haven't you put it on before? she asked
the mirror absently.

The answer came easily. Because she didn't wear
low-cut sweaters on dates, or skirts that kissed and
told on her figure. You don't advertise what you aren't
selling. The mirror was just full of answers she just
wasn't all that interested in hearing, so she turned
away from it. She was looking in the closet for her
black leather sandals when Johnny rapped on the door.

"I'm going over to Brian's now, Mom."

"Fine, honey. Have a good time." She emerged
from the closet three inches taller. "Be good?"

Her son gave her a lazy grin. "What's it worth?"

"To behave? Your hide." She gave him a swift kiss
and smile before heading back toward the dressing
table, first applying a moisturizer and then a subtle

mauve eyeshadow. Mascara and blusher, lip-stick . . . She glanced up again and saw Johnny still standing in the doorway. "What's wrong, sweetie?"

"Nothing." He dug his hands in his coat pockets. "You gonna be late tonight?"

"I don't know," Lorna answered truthfully. Her silky hair crackled under the vigorous brushing, gleaming like mahogany in the soft bedroom light; she drew it back with a small jet comb at her crown, then let the gleaming waves fall to her shoulders. The effect pleased her and she reached for a perfume bot-tle.

"That Matthew guy's been calling a lot. And you didn't go out with Hal last weekend, even though he called, too." Johnny hesitated, shifting his feet rest-lessly. Lorna knew he had more to say, but he wasn't saying it. "Watch yourself," he said finally, and promptly disappeared. A moment later Lorna heard the slam of the front door.

Watch yourself? She smiled ruefully. Who was taking care of whom in this household? She stood up, checking her image one last time in the mirror. The stark black sweater clung lovingly to her high breasts, showing off the pillow-soft flesh of her throat and her collarbones. The skirt stopped just below the knee, leaving a long expanse of shapely legs in dark, sheer stockings. Her eyes were a smoky gray, and her hair, freshly washed, radiated life, as well as the sheen of glossy chestnut. She felt feminine to her toes; the tingling of mixed anticipation and apprehension only increased when she saw the attractive reflection peer-ing back at her. Watch yourself, Lorna, she told the mirror wryly.

Laughing, Lorna carefully folded herself like an accordion into the narrow Morgan. "I feel as if I'm trying to fit my legs into a bumper car at a carnival!"

Matthew's automobile was a classic, dark green with a long, low front. When Lorna was seated, she could no longer see her toes, and she felt as if she were sitting an inch off the ground, although the rich leather seats were comfortable and the gadgets on the dashboard a study in luxury.

Matthew slammed the door on his side, effectively taking up all the rest of the available space and then some, and scowled at her. "If you insult my car, I guarantee it won't start."

Alarmed, Lorna promptly patted the dash. "Good baby, good baby." If the heat didn't come on soon, she was going to turn into an icicle. So much for open-weave skirts and bare throats.

Matthew grinned, giving her a sidelong glance as he turned the key in the ignition. When he'd called for her, he'd taken in every inch of her from the top of her head to her toes; she couldn't imagine why she flushed now. Because he was suddenly so close, she supposed. Because they both appeared to be rather taken aback at how startlingly fast, how *violently* fast, they seemed to be aware of each other in a completely new way. Because his dark coat and dark eyes and dark hair sent a starkly sexual message directly to her bloodstream. Because his shoulder was brushing hers, and because his hand on the gearshift was only inches from her thigh. Because...

"I hope you don't mind a little change in plans, Misha." The engine was purring smoothly now, and the car was cozy as toast.

She glanced at him. He had stopped at a stoplight, and reaching behind him brought forward two white bags, which he handed to her. She opened both, revealing two huge corned beef sandwiches, potato chips, pickles, and chocolate éclairs. Except for the pickles, she had no objections, but it was not exactly the kind of dinner she had dressed for.

"And we've only got ten minutes to eat." Seeing the expression she was trying so hard to hide, he chuckled. "It isn't exactly what I had planned, either. But unless you've changed your taste in music, Misha, I think you'll be pleased. I heard this afternoon that Oscar Peterson is going to be at the Bluebird for tonight only. So . . ."

"You're not serious."

"If you would rather just go to a nice restaurant, this stuff will keep."

She forced one of the sandwiches rapidly in his hand, not wasting any more time talking while she munched on her own. He chuckled again at her enthusiasm. She had no idea how he remembered her love of jazz; Richard hadn't liked it, and she had rarely played her cherished recordings while he was at home. She didn't care for avant-garde jazz, but she loved the traditional music, beginning with Bessie Smith in the twenties. She especially loved the type of song where the pianist picked up a love story and retold it in his own way, Oscar Peterson's specialty. She had heard Peterson twice in her life. She would practically have sold her soul to hear him a third time.

When Matthew stopped the car less than ten minutes later, Lorna opened her door before he could come around to do it for her. Impatiently, she lifted one foot and then the other, waiting while he locked the car on his side and approached hers. A light covering of snow blanketed the sidewalks, and the silvery flakes were still falling. She was shivering.

"Don't you ever wear boots?" he chided.

"Oh, stop it, Matthew. What time does Peterson start?"

"In seven minutes. We've still got time for a brisk walk around the block, if you—" He laughed at her horrified expression and draped a warm arm over her shoulder as they started walking. The swift kiss on her forehead startled her. "I was beginning to think you'd lost it, Misha. That little-kid ability to get all excited and just . . . be. Just laugh because of nothing at all."

She wasn't sure what he meant, and for an instant even resented the remark. Her life was a serious matter, not so very easy since the death of her father and the necessity of caring for Johnny by herself; surely Matthew didn't want or expect her to behave like a child? But that quick prick of resentment faded as she was warmed in the crook of his shoulder, matching his fast-paced walk. He was right in his way. She hadn't had such a simple feeling of sheer fun and anticipation in a long time.

A few minutes later, they walked down the steps to the basement nightclub that was the Bluebird. Stepping into darkness, Matthew took their coats while Lorna waited for her eyes to adjust. It would be euphemistic to call the place a dive. Old tables were crowded together over a faded linoleum floor; smoke was already filling the air; and the crowd was eclectic. Faded jeans mingled with gold lamé and a few black leather jackets; the single candle on each table illuminated trays of drinks waiting to be served. All chitchat stopped abruptly when the jazz trio started playing. No more drinks were served. The chatter of latecomers stopped at the doorway.

Lorna simply sat back, listened, and inhaled. Oscar Peterson was a middle-aged man, rather heavy, with skin the color of mahogany; by the second set sweat was pouring from his brow. He played from the soul, and the total silence in the place reflected his ability to reach the soul of his audience. The shabby room faded into something else; the group of mismatched individuals blended into appreciative afficianados under the spell of his music.

She wasn't aware how intently Matthew was watching her until the waitress served them drinks between the second and third sets. "I can tell you're having a rotten time," he murmured.

"Matthew..." She just looked at him, not knowing where to find the words to tell him how much the evening meant to her. She'd been afraid of a candlelit dinner, afraid they would suddenly be groping for conversation, afraid they would seem like strangers, afraid that special rapport she'd felt with him would disappear and that unhappy memories would poison the atmosphere, prevent any real communication between them. Now all that apprehension seemed unreal. How could she possibly feel uncomfortable when she knew Matthew shared her love of Peterson's music, when the evening had started out with hastily eaten sandwiches and there had been laughter from the start?

"You're so beautiful, Misha," he whispered. "When you're happy, you glow like a candle in a dark world. So easy to make happy, so easy to make sad. You touch your world, Misha—you make an impression on everyone who knows you. Did you know that?"

The place was dark and smoky, and the single candle on their table cast shadows on the planes of his face, adding a flicker of flame to his dark eyes when he looked at her. The music started again, yet this time Lorna felt drawn by a more potent magic than the subtle piano chords. Matthew's thigh rested against hers while they listened. His arm went around the back of the booth, his fingers absently resting on her shoulders, occasionally fondling her hair. His touch talked to her, whispering of the cocoon he wanted to spin around the two of them. When the trio started a low, haunting love song, there wasn't a sound in the place, and Lorna could feel the ache of old longings fill her as if she were a well that had been empty and hollow and cold and was now brimming with feelings so strong...

They left after midnight. The Ann Arbor streets were emptied of cars and totally silent. The glistening dark pavement and pure velvet covering of snow on the trees and grass made Lorna forget the frigid air that chilled her bones. She felt exhausted, exhilarated, high on music and recklessly exuberant as she hadn't been in months.

Matthew was laughing at something she said as he settled his rangy frame next to her in the Morgan. He dropped a swift, soft kiss on her mouth, so naturally that she was still smiling when he drew away to start the car. "Do you have to be home to accommodate a baby-sitter, or do you have time for a drink first?" he asked easily.

"Johnny's with Freda for the night, so I don't have to..." Her lighthearted smile faltered just a little, as reality came back with a little bump. Explaining that Johnny was off her hands for the night might sound like an open invitation, and she didn't need it spelled out to know Matthew was asking her to his place.

"Good, Misha. I had a feeling you weren't tired. I always have insomnia after a night of music," he drawled, looking straight ahead as he drove.

She looked at him. The sight of his strong profile under a street lamp sent a mental shiver down her spine. She swallowed. "I do, too, Matthew, but actually tomorrow I have to..."

"Work? So do I. But I want to talk to you, Misha. You don't really want to go home yet, do you?"

He had stopped for a red light, and turned to look at her. Stop melting, Lorna told herself sternly. You can't go into this just because you're in an insane mood and you're high on life for these few hours. But the look in Matthew's dark eyes seemed to touch her physically, to caress the silken strands of her hair, her soft lower lip, to rest on the vulnerable skin of her throat.

"Misha? I just want to talk," he assured her softly.

She settled back, staring straight ahead. "For one drink then," she agreed cautiously, but she thought, *Talk?* Matthew, you never used to be a liar.

CHAPTER
Five

"Your old place was so small next to this," Lorna said quietly, glancing around Matthew's condominium as he took her coat and she found a place for her purse on the hall table. She descended two thickly carpeted steps into the sunken living room, the decor a stark white and black, the lighting hidden, and the chrome gleaming. The interior decorator—obviously a professional had been at work here—had had an eye for luxury and elegance. The rich black carpeting and stark white couches were dramatic and masculine, with scarlet accents in the lacquered Chinese bar and a single high-backed chair.

"You don't like it," Matthew said from behind her.

"Of course I do."

"Misha."

"It's perfectly dreadful. Where on earth do you read the Sunday paper?"

He chuckled and motioned her to follow him with a crook of his little finger. "Come on and I'll show you where you can kick off your shoes. The room *does* work for entertaining..."

Entertaining *women,* she thought wryly. The couch was half the size of a bed. He led her down the hall, his palm in the hollow of her back, the only spot in her entire body that was warm after walking through the crisp snow from the car.

"More comfortable here?"

Slowly, she walked in ahead of him, deciding. She saw floor-to-ceiling bookshelves; and his desk was piled high with papers. Two long couches bordered the fireplace, both old and upholstered in brown tufted corduroy, faded a little and well worn. Wood was stacked in the hearth which still held a bed of ash, and above the fieldstone fireplace was an oil portrait of a flutist.

The painting instantly captured all of her attention. A black man in rags held a gilded flute in his hands. His eyes were closed as he played, suggesting that he could block out the loneliness and poverty and other insurmountable problems in the richness of his music. Lorna stared, mesmerized, and could have suddenly sworn she heard the same music she had listened to all evening. Until her eyes caught the flicker of flame. Matthew was lighting the fire.

"Will you pour us both a glass of wine, Misha? It's behind the desk there, in the credenza. I'm dying of thirst. I don't know how the two of us could have sat in a nightclub for more than three hours without finishing a single drink."

Obligingly, she moved behind the desk, glad to have something to do with her hands. "Who painted the portrait, Matthew?"

He glanced up at the oil painting. "An artist I met at a sidewalk sale at the art fair last summer. He was going to throw it away, said he didn't know how to finish it." He poked at a log, which tumbled over and sent a shower of orange sparks up the chimney. "I should have paid him a ton of money for it. I wanted to. But I was terrified that he would use it to go through art school and learn how to *finish* things." He stood up, pulling a wrought-iron screen in front of the fire. "You like it?"

"I covet it," she corrected wryly, as she poured wine from a decanter into two crystal glasses. "I feel I could walk down a crowded street and recognize the man in the portrait. Rich or poor, crook or saint, it wouldn't make any difference," she said whimsically, with just a trace of seriousness. "We all get desperate, day by day. Music helps me survive. At least, jazz does. Lets me forget absolutely everything else for a few minutes. Makes me feel free and in another world."

Matthew stripped off his tie as he took the wine from her and leaned back lazily against the mantel. "A few other things work just as well," he suggested, his dark eyes glinting on hers. She smiled softly as she settled in a corner of the couch.

"A good book?" she suggested, and watched that slash of a smile take over his face. She knew he'd meant making love, just as she knew he was about to make his first move. Wait, Matthew, she felt like saying. I know I came here of my own free will, but I really don't know; I haven't known anything since I walked into this house.

She needed a daisy, to peel off the petals and play the game. He was a stranger; he wasn't a stranger. She'd felt so easy with him all evening; she could almost believe they'd just met, that there were no unhappy memories of other people intruding on how they felt about each other. Every tiny physical contact was like a spark tempting love to flare up, threatening to explode . . . at least for her.

But this was not the man she'd known nine years ago. The silvery sideburns added an air of distinction to his looks that hadn't been there then; his whole apartment had a bachelor look to it that implied a man

who played a sophisticated game of seduction. The
Matthew she'd once known had been into work, day
and night. She wasn't at all sure how she felt coming
into his home as other women had undoubtedly come
over the years. Treated to wine and a fire and soft
lighting, she was on her guard.

"Were you in court today?" she asked idly.

He nodded, finally moving away from the fire and
settling on the couch across from her. "In court part
of the day, at the police station the rest." He smiled
wryly. "At times I wish I'd have gone into corporate
law, like Richard. At least those guys dress in suits
and take regular showers. I'm looking into an em-
bezzlement case; for the amount of money involved,
you'd think the client could have afforded deodorant."

Lorna's eyebrows shot up as she smiled. "You're
spoiling your image as a glamorous criminal attorney." He made a face. "You don't even sound as if
you think your client's innocent."

Matthew took a sip of wine and set his glass down,
stretching his long legs in front of him. "He's not—
but he's not guilty of all the charges against him,
either. He was just a little cog in a wheel too big for
him. There are times when I think half of all crime
comes down to the same thing. People in over their
heads and unable to find their way out . . ." He shook
his head. "When I first started out in this business of
the law, I wanted everyone to line up in neat little
categories: guilty or innocent."

"They don't," she suggested quietly.

He leaned forward, his eyes suddenly brooding,
the atmosphere abruptly no longer conducive to small
talk. "They don't," he echoed. "I work in the real
world, Misha. Every day the line is drawn finer.
There's right and wrong, yes. But innocent people
can commit an incredible number of moral crimes that
aren't punishable by law. And the guilty are often

tried only because they saw no alternative to breaking the law..."

He stopped abruptly and stared into the fire, then back at Lorna. "And I couldn't have my mind less on the law. Honey, I know damn well you're still hung up on what happened with my brother."

The unexpected change from theoretical law to their personal past threw her. She set down her glass. "Matthew..."

"You never committed a crime, Misha," he said quietly. "I raised Richard, from the time our mother died. I knew him, and I loved my brother. That's not to say I ever thought him incapable of making a mistake. He was in over his head, wanting success all at once, and he dragged you into that complicated maelstrom. I did the best I could by him, Misha, and I'll be damned if I'll acknowledge guilt for the way I feel about you now."

"Matthew..." Her throat was suddenly dry.

"Please listen to me, Misha," he grated, leaning forward. His expression was steely and his eyes were haunted, intensely pinning hers. "I don't want the shadow of the past between us, Misha. I want to hear from you that it isn't there. When I walked into my office and found you waiting there, I could see that you were expecting me to lash out at you, and I don't understand why. I never judged you. It was a long time ago, and, honey, you're not the only woman— or man—to make that particular mistake." His voice softened. "Besides, you've paid a hell of a price over the years for being nineteen once upon a time. For being a little too beautiful, a little too young, a little too lonely."

But he believed she had been unfaithful. Her stomach was suddenly churning with turbulent emotions. "Matthew, you think you understand—"

"No. Not understand. I'm trying to tell you that I don't give a damn. It's past, unless it's still affecting you now. You sought *me* out, Misha. And if that had anything to do with leftover feelings for my brother—"

"God, no." Lorna jumped up from the couch, folding her arms slowly across her chest, turning away so he couldn't see her rapidly blinking away tears. "I don't still love or hate your brother, Matthew. That's what you're asking me? Not for a long time. It has nothing to do with why I came to see you."

It was Johnny, she thought achingly. She had wanted the security of the Whitaker family for her son. That was the reason she had gone to see Matthew, but instead of solving the problem, her action had created a new one. Problem? It had always mattered so much what Matthew thought of her, that he not judge her harshly. And he saw with such compassion what she had been unable to forgive in herself, that she had been a too-young, too-lonely nineteen. He understood that, but not what counted to her. She closed her eyes, and then turned to face him. "Maybe what I feel now is crazy," she admitted quietly. "Because I don't believe you, Matthew. I want to, but I don't believe that you've forgotten, that you don't care. You still think I'm the kind of woman who would be unfaithful—"

He sucked in his breath and stood up restlessly. She saw a flash of something stark and brilliant in his eyes before she turned away to stare into the fire. From behind her, she felt his hands suddenly massage the nape of her neck, a gentle, soothing caress, his fingers intuitively discovering every knotted muscle. Only gradually did his hands leave her neck and trail down to her waist, pulling her gently back against him, his soft kiss on her cheek simple, slow, and easy. "I'm not a boy," he said quietly. "And you're not that kind of woman, Misha. There would be no chance of your being unfaithful to me. Do you want me to show you?"

The fire was sending golden sparks up the chimney. There was no reason for the vulnerable little shiver that rippled through her body. "No," she whispered.

He was behind her, but she could feel his smile, his amusement that she was suddenly shying like a fawn. His arms tightened around her, securing her in the cocoon of his embrace, a cherishing, protective embrace that touched off a thousand nerve endings. And confused her, totally. "Yes," he said softly. "Yes, Misha. Let me touch you. Let me show you..."

She could not seem to turn around and face him. Matthew didn't appear to care. His cheek nudged aside her hair so that his lips could find her soft skin. There, where the nape of her neck burned. Her throat, the hollow in her shoulder... she was *not* the kind of woman to go to bed with a man because of a simple attraction. She was not some wanton to whom vows of love meant nothing. She'd never been driven by libido in her life. It was terribly important that Matthew understand that, that he respect her, that he trust her...

"The minute I saw you," he murmured, "I wanted to hold you, Misha. To touch you, to feel your touch. I wanted to hear your laughter; I wanted to watch you listening to music; I wanted to scold you for wearing sandals in the coldest weather. I wanted you beside me in the night..."

"Matthew..." She closed her eyes, arching her head back as his lips continued to tease and savor at the side of her throat. He leaned against the back of the couch, pulling her into the cradle of his thighs, his lips finding ample territory to explore in the flesh laid bare by the scooped neck of her sweater. Collarbone and throat, the silky hollow just below her ear, the fragile cords of her neck.

She suddenly felt as weak as a kitten, and strangely reluctant to open her eyes. Despair shot through her, mingled with desire. For Johnny's sake, for her own, she knew she could not leave Matthew believing as he did. It mattered so much! She tried to think, and couldn't. Her blood was singing in her veins, a song of blues and rhythm that was all she seemed to hear. She felt enfolded in velvet-encased iron, her back cradled against his chest, her bottom cradled into his thighs, his arms around her. His hands caressed the cashmere covering her abdomen, over and over, as restless as his lips at her throat. "Misha..."

It was like a low call from the back of his throat, a sweet whisper to follow him, his music, his magic. His hands slid up and crossed to knead the aching swells of her breasts. Her heart beat so loudly that she knew he could hear it. She opened her eyes and saw the shadows the fire was casting on the wall, saw his dark head bent over her. Her own head arched back in the curve of his shoulder as his hands moved over her body. She could smell cherry wood and leather and the dry wine from his lips, could smell Matthew...

"Misha," he murmured again, and turned her, his lips sealing in a message of sweet, driving hunger. Her hands clutched his hair, forcing the kiss to deepen. She hurt. Deep in her loins she felt the most unbearable pain, so consuming it frightened her.

He pulled the sweater loose from the waistband of her skirt, and the touch of his warm palm on her abdomen seared, sent a shiver through her body. He seemed to love that shiver. She could feel the change in her breathing and the increase in fevered pressure on her mouth, in the dominating way he drew her closer, possessively wrapping his arms around her. He wanted her trembling. And it was so easy to give him what he wanted.

He unfastened the button on the waist of her skirt. The fabric slid lazily down her silk-clad hips. Her arms were already raised to his neck, and he easily slipped the sweater off. For just a moment, the black cashmere blinded her, going over her head, and for just that moment she groped for a fraction of sanity. "No," she protested.

Matthew draped the sweater over the back of the couch and savored the look of her. The black slip was simple, lace free, a smooth satiny fabric that molded itself to her figure. His eyes met hers, all black and fierce fire. "Nothing on earth could stop me from making love to you, Misha," he whispered. "Nothing except you."

She took a breath, her heart beating frantically, and stared at him. His hands were slowly moving up and down her sides, absorbing the feel and look of silk against her skin. Those hands were suddenly lazy, waiting. And Lorna had thousands of vocabulary words in four languages to choose from at the tip of her tongue. *Nyet. Non. Nein.* Please, Matthew...

Slowly, his hands shifted down from her waist, resting possessively on the curve of her hips. "Unbutton my shirt, Misha," he whispered.

The buttons trembled beneath her fingers. "Matthew. Listen..." Would he settle for a brilliant discussion of world politics? Because somewhere in her head she knew this wasn't right. It was too fast, too overwhelming, too unsettled... Yet another corner of her mind told her that nothing could be more right. No one else had made her feel like this. She'd said no to men for years because she had felt it wasn't right. And Matthew was no stranger. Once friend...now lover. And when her hands climbed up the warm flesh of his chest, she could anticipate his shudder even before she felt it.

"Misha..."

The lazy sensuality in his eyes was replaced by something yet more compelling. She was still absorbing that look in his eyes as he lowered her to the carpet, a long powerful leg stealing between hers, pressing intimate flesh against intimate flesh. She closed her eyes as he removed her slip and unclasped her bra. He buried her low, guttural murmur in her throat with his lips on hers, draining her mouth of sound. The feeling of her bare breasts crushed to his chest touched off a summons in her soul, a burst of desire so consuming...

The fire was such a bright orange, licking flames up the flue. Matthew's flesh took on the silk sheen of moisture; the fire was reflected in his eyes, which seemed to blacken to ebony at her fevered touch. She could not touch enough, as she watched the sheen of his teak skin, seeing the shadows of both of them in the movements of love, seeing the flames burn higher. Lovingly, they finished undressing one another, and she clasped his naked body to hers.

He whispered her name over and over as she took him inside her, trembling with that intimate intrusion, murmuring a sudden startled cry. She was someone else, a stranger, bursting with an aching, restless need so intense that she felt lost, frightened. For so long, she had trusted no one; for so long she had allowed no one to come close; never had she felt so vulnerable. She wanted Matthew so desperately. Too much. *Love me, Matthew. Make it all right*...

His hand brushed back her hair, over and over. "Easy," he murmured. "I'm going nowhere without you, love. Nowhere. You know better. You're going with me. Trust me..."

She barely heard the words, with his lips in her

hair, but she could feel in his body language what he was trying to say. The tension had come from nowhere. A butterfly fleeing the sound of the wind; a wild creature that bolted from fear of being captured. And Matthew remained cleaved to her, his body part of her own. His warm weight absorbed her trembling; his hands moved slowly, with infinite tenderness; his lips made slow, patient, infinite promises. She could have sworn he understood her better than she understood herself. A long time ago, she had been deserted in a time of need she would never forget; in fierce, wild passion, she had forgotten that. Her soul hadn't, not at the time when she was at her most vulnerable, when there could be no fulfillment without trust.

"Matthew . . ."

His touch, so tender, kindled fresh fire. His murmured words kindled more; the scent of him, the feel of his skin, the promise in his eyes . . . The complicated problems in her life suddenly seemed so simple. Every instinct told her he loved her. Every instinct responded to that promise. With touch, with love, with flame, she responded, and he gave back in kind. It was double what they had started out with. He had taken a wild, fiercely abandoned woman to a very special place, where no one could ever have heard such music, where no one could ever have been made so free.

Sleepily, she curled next to him. Matthew pressed kiss after kiss on her temples, in her hair; both of them exhausted in the aftermath of loving. "So warm, Misha, so incredibly lovely." His finger gently nudged up her chin so he could look at her again. "You glow, did you know that? All giving . . ."

She shook her head, flushing faintly.

He smiled, just as faintly, bemused at her shyness.

"Can I tell you what a beautiful body you have?" He murmured teasingly.

She shook her head again.

"What an incredible lover you are? What I felt like when I was inside you? I never wanted to leave you, sweet. I never wanted it to end. It was as if I'd always known how it could be and I couldn't stand to let go of you . . ."

She snuggled her cheek in the crook of his shoulder, her arms still loosely around his neck. He kissed her again, rubbing his face against her cheek until she smiled, feeling ticklish, forgetting her shyness.

"On the other hand . . ." He nudged up her chin again so he could look in her eyes. "I'm not too pleased at getting quite so carried away. There are four couches in this house and three beds, Misha. Would you like to tell me how we ended up on the carpet?"

That roused her, her lips irrepressibly curling up at the corners. "You're a disgrace as a sophisticated bachelor," she said gravely. "What good are all the recessed lights and the elegant couches if you're really a teenager with a libido that gets ahead of you? Honestly, Matthew. What happened to all that formidable control, the authoritative decision-maker . . ."

"It's all your fault," he growled.

"Yours."

He shook his head. "I couldn't think. It was your fault I couldn't think."

"That's your business, thinking. Brilliantly outthinking criminals."

"No, I outthink prosecuting attorneys."

He chuckled and leaned over her, placing a languid kiss exactly between her third and fourth rib. "What's criminal, Misha, is what you do to me. How you took fire . . ."

And she had, she thought fleetingly. But it had never been like that before. Never had she associated lovemaking with such intense passion, such abandoned fire, such desperate need, such perfect synchrony. She'd learned the rules with Richard a very long time ago, but had never played the game. At nineteen, she had known nothing about loving. She remembered suddenly how much she had lost then, and realized with frightening awareness how much more she could lose now.

She was falling in love with Matthew, and that made her more vulnerable than she had ever been in her life.

It was four in the morning; the fire had died; the air grew cool on her skin; and all she wanted to do was sleep. Instead, she admitted to herself that it was past time to go home.

CHAPTER
Six

"MOM!"

Lorna's eyes flew open, focused vaguely and rejected the harsh winter sunlight beaming down on her bed; then she closed them again.

"Mom! Aren't you even going to thank me for letting you sleep in until eight o'clock?"

Eight o'clock? When she hadn't gotten to bed until five? Her eyes stayed closed against the virtuous appeal in her son's voice. Johnny hesitated.

"I tell you what. I'll make us both breakfast—"

Resolutely, she pushed the covers off her body, freezing-cold air replacing her warm cocoon and forcing wakefulness on her. The last time Johnny had volunteered to prepare breakfast Lorna had spent four hours cleaning up. "I'll make it," she said groggily. "You want pancakes or bacon and eggs?"

"French toast."

Naturally. She stumbled over to the closet, shrugged on a robe and slippers, and joined her son in the kitchen. She put butter in the skillet to melt while she dipped the thick pieces of French bread in beaten egg, her head feeling distinctly like steel wool. Old steel wool. Johnny's usual Saturday-morning exuberance was enough to make her wince. There was something about a weekend that always seemed to bring out the restlessness in a child. Cartoons were blaring from a television set in the other room; a fleet of matchbox cars stood in a line on the kitchen table; and for some unknown reason Johnny was tossing a football up in the air as if the snow weren't three inches thick outside.

"Freda says if you want me off your hands for the day, she's willing to take the two of us over to the Science Institute. There's a thing there about whales. Then maybe she'll take us Christmas shopping. Can I go?"

"Sure." Lorna smiled at him as she set his plate on the table. "Only not like that."

"Like what?"

She explained patiently. "Your socks don't match, that sweat shirt has three holes in it, and your jeans are patched. Why don't you put on your gray pants."

He made a face as if she'd suggested he take castor oil. She sat down across from him and took a life-giving draught of coffee. She was actually waking up, more the pity.

Matthew was miles away, undoubtedly sleeping in the expensive condominium where he must have taken his share of women to sleep with him over the years. Women who didn't have to wake him up in the middle of the night to take them home to their offspring. The evening of music and laughter and lovemaking seemed a year ago, a precious dream.

Reality was a cramped orange and almond kitchen, a towhead son with a cowlick, a houseful of toys to clean up, and a translating job to do this morning. Guilt was raging in her head like an out-of-control fever, alternating with shame, as she poured herself a second cup of coffee. How *could* she have forgotten Johnny? How *could* she have slept with Matthew, the first evening they'd spent together, acting just as loose as he'd thought she was when she was nineteen? Was that any way to build trust? Matthew had nothing to lose in an affair, while she had everything to lose. Her self-respect, for example. Johnny could be pulled into the middle...

"What are you so quiet for?" Johnny demanded, with his mouth full of food. "Were you out late last night?"

"I came in early, actually," Lorna answered. Which was, of course, the truth. Early this morning.

"Was he nice to you?"

Lorna stood up and took her son's empty plate to the counter. "Very nice. We heard some music," she said flatly. *Please leave it, sweetheart.*

Johnny studied her covertly as he swiped at his mouth with a napkin. She could visualize the slight frown on his forehead even if she wasn't directly looking at him. Oversensitive as he was, she knew Johnny sensed that something differentiated Matthew from the other men she had dated. He just didn't quite know what to do about it. "How come you let me call him Matthew?" he asked finally. "Everyone else, it's supposed to be Mister this or Mister that."

She forced herself to look directly at her son. "His last name is Whitaker, Johnny. Didn't I mention it?" His jaw dropped, with a host of questions all ready. She thought, I can't handle this. "It isn't as common a name as Smith, but it's not uncommon either. It just happens we all share the last name." If he asked her directly if they were related, she would probably cry. Though she didn't feel ready to tell him the whole truth, she could not conceive of telling her son a blatant lie. See what you got into, she told her conscience.

"You gonna see him again?" Johnny asked.

"I may."

He sighed, scowling at her petulantly. Lorna usually had more laughter and conversation for him; she enjoyed her son. He got up from the kitchen chair to go back into his bedroom to change for his outing, but he hesitated, fidgeting in the doorway. "Did he like me, Mom?" he asked carefully. "I mean, from the time he had dinner with us."

Her heart wrenched, tying itself up in knots. "Did I get my morning hug, urchin?" she asked suddenly, and claimed it, wrapping her arms around her son and holding him tightly, until he squirmed. He grinned up at her.

"You two don't know each other well enough to like or dislike each other, Johnny," she said. "It doesn't matter. Nothing to worry about. You come first with me, got that? Nothing and no one is ever going to make a difference for us. Now go change your clothes before Freda gets here."

At one that afternoon Lorna was driving on a winding country road called Pontiac Trail. Sunlight glinted off the snowy landscape, creating a glare that made it difficult to read the numbers on the mailboxes. Directions weren't Lorna's strong point at the best of times, but on her third pass she located 2257 and turned into the narrow gravel drive.

She stopped the car a hundred yards farther on, rather surprised at the stables and brand-new A-frame in front of her. From the crisp, cultured voice of the man she'd spoken to on the phone, she'd rather idly expected an ivy-covered cottage and an English garden—covered with snow.

Stepping from the car, she automatically checked to make sure her chignon was in place and her coat neat, then snatched up her small briefcase and headed toward the door. It opened just as she raised her hand to push the bell. "Mrs. Whitaker? I was beginning to worry about you."

"Make it Lorna, please, and I'm terribly sorry I'm late. It's not that I didn't start out in plenty of time—"

"It doesn't matter. Let me get you a cup of coffee. I'd like to talk to you for a minute before you meet my mother."

"Fine."

He took her coat, escorted her to a pine-paneled contemporary living room, and brought coffee a moment later. Lorna studied the man absently while he poured her a cup of the dark brew. His name was Stan Valicheck. He looked to be in his early forties, a spare, neat man, wearing loose corduroy pants in the European style and a navy-blue crew-neck sweater. He had kind eyes, something Lorna always noticed first in a person, and their brown color almost exactly matched the shade of his hair.

"My mother used to know your father; that's why I looked you up, Lorna. I think I told you that on the phone..."

Lorna nodded, aware she was being thoroughly assessed. He seemed to approve of her simple cranberry wool slacks and matching sweater; she could tell that he liked the neat chignon. She guessed he was single from the speculation in his eyes, but there was nothing offensive about his perusal. He moved easily, as if he'd never had a trace of nerves in his life.

He sat down across from her. "For three years, my mother's been working on this book, about her childhood in Russia. I just let her be; it gave her something to do. She's been lonely in this country, what with the language barrier."

"I understand," Lorna said compassionately.

He nodded, smiling wryly. "But now that she's done with the manuscript, she's intent on getting it published. Frankly, Lorna, I haven't the least idea if it's excellent or terrible; I can't read a word of Russian. To please her, I'm willing to have it translated. I didn't want to discuss the fees with you on the phone because I wanted to explain. What I had in mind was a flat five thousand. If by some chance the story proves to be worth something, I'd be willing to add to that. I'm trying to be honest with you, though; there's no counting on more. And just as frankly, I couldn't care less about the financial success of the venture; I have only my mother's happiness on my mind. And maybe preserving the story of her past for posterity."

Lorna leaned forward, touched by his attitude toward his mother. "Please understand, I'm grateful for the chance to work on this. I've written sewing-machine instructions in four languages, composed travel brochures, described computers and electronics component systems, but I've never translated literature, and frankly, I may not even be qualified. I am enthusiastic about the project, though, because I was raised on Russian folklore and the Russian feeling for life. Through my father. And I'd like to tell you I would put your mother's book before everything else. But as I said on the phone, I do have regular commitments."

And Matthew's nest egg was bothering her, though obviously she couldn't tell Stan Valicheck that. In principle that was money due Johnny, but emotionally, Lorna still felt unhappy about it, guilty that she hadn't been able to salt away any savings on her own. Security mattered; she never knew how much until her father died, until she was alone with no one to turn to when Johnny needed something she couldn't provide. With this job, even if she had to work nights to fit it in with her other commitments, she could either put her earnings in the bank or begin to pay back Matthew.

They talked a few more minutes before Stan stood up, smiling warmly at her. "Time to take you up to meet Mother, then." He hesitated. "You're an awfully pretty lady for someone who spends hours buried behind foreign-language dictionaries. Are you married, Lorna?"

"Divorced. With a nine-year-old son," she answered, setting down her cup and gathering up her briefcase to follow him.

"I know you'll be working at your home, but Mother will be counting on you to report in from time to time. You're welcome to bring the boy. We have horses in back—"

"I noticed." Lorna felt something chafe at her nerve endings. Stan obviously liked children; he was a kind man, not bad looking. She didn't know his profession, but the house hadn't been put together on a shoestring. A father for Johnny. The thought clicked automatically in her head; it was the same thought that had colored her judgment of men for years. Until she'd met Matthew again. Last night's lovemaking lingered in her head, yet she brought herself sharply back to the present, forcing the memory away. One of the thousand things she seemed to have forgotten last night was that Matthew, up to this point, could barely tolerate hearing Johnny's name mentioned. "I'd like to bring my son," she admitted slowly, and glanced at Stan. "But I don't want to jump to any conclusions. For one thing, your mother might not even like me, and as I just told you I've never had the chance to do this kind of work before."

"She'll love you," Stan assured her, as if he couldn't imagine anyone who didn't.

Anna Valicheck was in her late sixties, but she looked ninety. Her son had not inherited her heavy features. Her stark white hair was drawn back in a severe bun; her legs were covered with a blanket to hide arthritic limbs. The two women drank tea from a samovar, chatted in Russian of history and literature and Lorna's father. The thick, handwritten manuscript was in Lorna's lap, and though she was itching to look at it, there was no time. Anna was lonely for the ease and comfort of being able to talk in her own tongue; Lorna couldn't deny her.

Lorna loved her. The woman had grown up in Siberia, where her father had been exiled for political activism, both a sad and dramatic story that was the basis for her "diary," as she called it. She evinced no self-pity. She had an acerbic tongue, and a dramatic way of speaking that was uniquely Russian. Lorna, raised on Eastern fairy tales, could appreciate Anna's collection of enameled and jeweled eggs more than someone who never knew their origins. They both forgot the time as they talked, until Lorna looked up in surprise to find Stan in the doorway, smiling with humorous affection at both of them.

"Now, I told Lorna we would take an hour of her time, and here it is five o'clock," he scolded his mother.

"But you cannot leave," Anna told Lorna. "You will stay for dinner."

Lorna stood up, smiling. Truthfully, she would have loved to stay for dinner. She felt a spontaneous warmth toward both Anna and Stan, as if they were old friends rather than potential clients. But she shook her head regretfully. "I appreciate the invitation, but I'm sorry—I really can't."

"Of course you can," Stan insisted.

She shook her head again, not explaining that she had left Johnny with a sitter the night before and that she never did that two evenings in a row. She got to her feet, shifting the heavy manuscript in her arms.

"I promise to come back and see you, though, if I may," she told Anna.

Stan walked her to the car, carrying the manuscript and her briefcase. "I haven't seen my mother so animated in years. She's usually extremely reticent with strangers."

"So am I," Lorna admitted with a little laugh. "You two were so nice...I don't know what I expected when you called. I think I was afraid you would take one look at me and decide you needed an older, more professorial type to translate the story. And I was desperately afraid the manuscript would be in Ukrainian. I really would have had a hard time handling that..."

"I doubt you could have a hard time handling anything." He opened the door for her, and she slid in behind the steering wheel.

"I'll need a chance to read it through before I can really commit myself to this or give you an estimate of how long it will take me to do it," she said seriously, increasingly aware his brown eyes grew warmer the longer he looked at her.

"And that will take you how long?"

Unconsciously, she bit her lip, thinking. "I should be able to look it over by next Wednesday."

"Would it be better if I called at your house late Wednesday afternoon, then?" He added smoothly, "If you should find problems, I would rather discuss them with you first, without my mother knowing."

In terms of business, his suggestion was reasonable, though Lorna knew he was creating the opportunity simply to see her again. She didn't know what to say for a minute, and then decided her hesitation was ridiculous. This was no heavy-handed man-on-the-make; she had a perfectly legitimate reason for seeing him, and he was nice. He'd gone out of his way to boost her morale from the moment she'd walked in the door, in an easy, inoffensive way. "All right," she agreed, but there was no stopping the niggling guilt in the back of her mind. She refused to put Matthew's name on it.

She closed the door and waved good-bye as Stan stepped back and then turned toward the house. Putting the car in gear, she backed up, and sighed as she drove the winding curves of Pontiac Trail again. It was the most pleasant, carefree afternoon she had had in weeks. Mentally, she gave herself a pat on the back. She had only thought of Matthew 597 times.

When Lorna got home, she made dinner for Johnny, who for the next two hours harangued her with reasons why she could no longer buy Finnish, Russian, or Japanese goods; it seemed those three countries persisted in hunting whales that were on the endangered species list. Her son's commitment to the cause made her smile, although Lorna knew better than to treat the subject lightly. She did point out to him that the economies of those countries were heavily dependent on fishing, but Johnny was not to be discouraged. Nor could he be dissuaded from packing up a near fortune in matchbox cars that happened to have been made in Japan.

A little later, Lorna called Freda. "Thanks for taking him," she said, with a touch of irony in her voice.

Freda laughed into the phone. "Has he bashed in the record player yet, or are all its parts American-made? I tried to explain to him that there was another side to the story, that those people might have to fish to live and you just couldn't take away their livelihood—"

"I did, too." Lorna added thoughtfully, "He said there had to be an answer for that. And just because the answer was hard was no excuse to do something wrong—as in killing the animals, upsetting the balance of nature."

"He's something, your son."

Lorna agreed, hung up a short time later, and went into the living room where Johnny was sprawled with both legs over the arm of the chair and a book in his hands. "Bedtime, Johnny." Amid his groans and protests, she herded him into the other room, bullied him into picking up his clothes and harassed him until he washed his hands and face. When he was lying in his bed and looking like a perfect angel, he informed her that he was going to have power when he grew up. Power enough to right all the injustices in the world.

She bent down to kiss him, brushing back the cowlick. "I love you, Johnny," she said quietly, turned out the light, and left the room. He sounded so much like a Whitaker that she could have cried. Justice, right and wrong; at nine years old he was already struggling to do the right thing . . . as he perceived it.

Lorna took a bath, did a little cleaning up, then sat in the darkened living room for a long time. She was exhausted, and every hour since she had left Matthew had added to the confusion and guilt in her mind. She felt resentful, unsettled as a butterfly, and unsure— as she seemed to have felt unsure her entire life—as to what the right and wrong of certain decisions were. Johnny, like Matthew, found the issues so easy to deal with. At the moment, the only conclusion she could come to was that it would be better not to see Matthew for a while. Even if he called.

He called. She heard the phone and ran for it, not wanting Johnny to wake up. "Misha?"

She heard the low, husky baritone, and her stomach flipped over. She caught her breath, feeling like a perfect fool. "It's me, Matthew," she confirmed. She knew her voice sounded cool and distant, disguising the anxiety that had plagued her all day. Her heart, by contrast, was soaring at the simple sound of his voice.

"You've been upset, haven't you?" he asked quietly, but it was not really a question. "Misha, it was too soon. I know that. I didn't intend..." He hesitated, as if waiting for her to say something she couldn't seem to say. "I didn't take you out to rush you into bed. I just wanted to see you again. To be with you..." He hesitated again, and still she didn't answer. "I called to tell you I was sorry I rushed things, but on the other hand I can't quite seem to do that. I loved last night... Misha..." He paused again, and a thread of humor suddenly entered his voice. "You wouldn't like to help me with this conversation, would you?"

Helplessly, she heard a low throaty chuckle escape her throat, matched by his.

"Say hello, Matthew," he ordered into the phone.

"Hello, Matthew," she obeyed softly.

"I'm going to come and see you when I can get free next week. We'll walk, Misha. Out in the snow. Nowhere near carpets and firelight. Do you hear me?"

She heard him. And she dreamed all night of making love on the carpet in front of the fire.

CHAPTER
Seven

THE OAK OFFICE chair had never quite felt comfortable to Lorna; she usually padded it with a pillow. Two if she was typing. At the moment, she was sitting on it crosswise, her legs slung over one arm, a blue pencil between her teeth and a red one stuck behind her ear.

It had been snowing outside since early that morning, though she'd barely noticed. Yellow legal-pad pages had been skimming off her lap and onto the gnarled walnut desk since first light. At one, she'd stopped reluctantly to eat a sandwich; it was now a little after two.

By working Sunday and the last three nights on her regular work, she'd made time for Anna's manuscript. She was in love with it. With the red pencil she kept track of grammatical problems she would have to resolve in translating from Russian to English, while she used the blue pencil to mark passages where she had questions about the meaning. She would have to ask Anna Valicheck to explain those to her. There were dozens of marks, red and blue, throughout the yellow pages.

Lorna stopped her reading, shoved her reading glasses to the top of her head, and rubbed her tired eyes. She badly needed a break but was too engrossed in the story to take one. Blinking hard, she stared restlessly out at the huge flakes of snow falling on the windowsill, then just as absently focused her gaze on the small hole in her thick gray socks. The matching gray wool slacks were old, baggy, and maybe a little too well loved over the years. The oversized red flannel shirt fit loosely over her breasts. It was her favorite outfit for a dig-in winter workday. She stretched lazily to get the kinks out of her taut muscles, and heard the doorbell ring.

Frowning impatiently at the interruption, she padded around the desk to the front hall. Opening the door, she had to blink hard against the sudden brilliant glare of snow brightness, and felt the sharp edge of a cardboard box jab into her stomach for her trouble.

"It's falling, Misha, watch it!"

"Matthew!" The box tumbled to the floor while she was staring at him. Somewhere above several other white cardboard boxes were his disarming dark eyes and a special mischievous smile that took her breath away. Snow glinted in his hair, was already layered on the shoulders of his coat. "What on earth——"

"We're going for a walk. I *told* you," he reminded her, coming inside and closing the door behind him, "but then, knowing you, I realized what a foolish idea that was. The snow's six inches deep, and I've never seen you in anything but bare feet or ridiculously flimsy sandals."

He straightened up after setting the boxes on the carpet. For a moment, Lorna almost thought he was nervous, the way he was chattering, but being Matthew . . . well, he just couldn't be. *She* was the one, whipping the glasses off her head, groping to extricate the red pencil from her hair. And suddenly Matthew

was laughing, finding the blue pencil still stuck in her
ponytail, releasing her hair from the taut rubber band,
running his hands through the chestnut waves. "Before
we go for a walk," he teased, "maybe I'd better see
a birth certificate. I don't want to be arrested for
statutory rape."

"Matthew, I don't want to tell you that you're out
of your mind," she said, "but this is not exactly the
day for a walk."

"No," he agreed. Before she realized what was
happening, he'd gently tugged her hair back, tilting
her face up to his. His lips swept over hers roughly,
their texture freezing cold and unbelievably soft. Ever
so tenderly his palms cupped her face, lingering there.
"It's a day for curling up on a carpet in front of a
fire," he said huskily, and then his voice hardened.
"We're going for a walk. Hustle up and open the
boxes."

Inside she felt like melted butter, but she made a
monumental effort not to show it. "It's the middle of
the afternoon. Aren't you supposed to be working?"
She remembered, *"I'm* supposed to be working." Only
a few moments earlier, she recalled, she'd been de-
lightfully, wholeheartedly absorbed in Anna's mem-
oirs.

"See?" He bent down to toss the lid off one box,
dredging up one heavily fur-lined boot. "I would have
bought size six and a half, since that's what you used
to say you wore. But I got a seven and a half so there
was a chance they'd fit." He chuckled at the instant
crimson flush on her cheeks, then trailed a soft white
angora scarf around her neck, and reached in the third
box for a matching angora hat. He put it on her head
and tucked in her hair without the least concern for
style.

His fingers, Lorna realized, were trembling. She
stood, frozen, as he fitted a pair of fur-lined gloves

on her hands. The gifts bewildered her; Matthew's whirlwind arrival bewildered her. Even more disconcerting was the way he kept avoiding her eyes. When he turned, she saw that his profile was dark and intense . . . Matthew *was* nervous. Did he honestly believe she would turn him away?

"Matthew . . ."

But there was no trace of anxiety on his face when he finally looked at her. Just a slash of a smile and a rather bossy chin. "Come on, Misha. Put on the boots so you can fib and tell me how big they are."

She did. "They're huge," she announced. Just the tiniest bit snug in one toe.

"We'll leave that," he said dryly. "Now I suppose it's too much to expect that you own a warm coat."

She was bundled up like a mummy before he was satisfied. They walked toward the university campus. Matthew kept his gloved hands in his pockets, never touching her. The snow continued to fall steadily, big pure flakes that coated their clothes and occasionally lingered on their eyelashes, their faces. Lorna could feel her cheeks turn crimson, and welcomed the crisp, cold air in her lungs.

"Are you cold?" he asked her once.

She shook her head, and they didn't talk after that. The campus was crowded with kids milling around between classes, battling the snowy walks. They all looked alike, with their army jackets and jeans, ruddy cheeks, and armloads of books. She and Matthew always appeared to be walking against the tide, no matter which direction they took. Everyone else seemed to be chattering and laughing, while she and Matthew just shared an occasional glance or spontaneous smile.

In the corner of the campus was an arboretum. In spring and summer, the wooded glen was lush and green, with a long, sloping meadow where students usually had to reserve spots for their blankets. Mat-

thew lifted her over a snowbank. Breathing in deeply,
she looked around as he vaulted up behind her. The
meadow was a long, low carpet of white diamonds,
without a single footprint to mar the treasure of a
landscape. Stark black tree trunks rose in little se-
cluded coves...It was like entering another world.
If there were cars only a block away, she couldn't
hear them. They were no longer part of the city; there
were no people, no other sounds.

Still they walked, until they reached a stand of
trees. There, Matthew finally stopped, leaning back
against a fat black walnut tree, his head resting against
the bark. He wore no hat; his hair was damp, and his
face had reddened with the cold, and his beautiful
eyes were looking into hers.

She leaned back against an opposite tree and studied him, saying nothing. He had made her feel this
way at the nightclub, and he was doing it now. Somehow just being with him gave her the feeling that there
were only the two of them in the world. They were
the only two who had *really* heard the seductive jazz,
the only two who really took a walk together, the only
two who really made love. Obviously, no one else
had ever done these things. Poor world, she felt like
saying.

She couldn't imagine how this could be the same
man she had known nine years ago. He had touched
her life then, but never colored it. Whereas now...

"We've got to talk, Misha," he said softly.

She nodded, starting to come toward him. "We
have to talk," she agreed. "Tell me what you were
really supposed to be doing this afternoon?"

"Nothing that matters. Since Dad retired, I've taken
on three new attorneys in the office. I'm thinking
about hiring another. All *I* would have done this afternoon was sit in a chair with my feet up and read *Field
and Stream...*"

So the Whitakers had been busy expanding and Matthew was still working long hours... and he had nevertheless taken the time to come and see her. Lorna moved closer, pulling off her gloves and shoving them in her pockets. Finger by finger, she removed his then, before raising her arms to his shoulders. She had to go up on tiptoe to kiss him, irresistibly impelled to touch his cold cheeks, to rub her smooth, cold lips against his. They were both padded with clothes from the neck down, a chastity cushion teasingly forbidding them the kind of contact they both craved. A sudden swift breeze sent a light shower of snow cascading down onto their shoulders from the bare tree branches. It didn't seem to matter. Lorna had never felt so warm.

Matthew stood very still, not responding to her kiss, though not drawing away. His eyes had darkened the moment she touched him. "I told my father I was seeing you."

She stepped back abruptly, her troubled eyes seeking his, yet Matthew radiated no concern. It was something he wanted her to know, answering one of many questions for her before she had even asked it... Yet the subject no longer seemed of any interest to him. He reached out to cradle her throat with his palms, his thumbs caressing the cold, soft skin of her cheek. Gradually, his fingers pushed back her hat, letting her hair tumble to her shoulders, and suddenly his hands were lost in the luxuriant waves as he gathered her close. "Misha..." Her eyes closed as his mouth came down on hers.

The world obligingly decelerated to slow motion. The swift breeze slowed; a single snowflake lingered on her cheek. His lips warmed against hers; her fingers lazily memorized the texture of his hair. The leisurely intrusion of his tongue between her teeth was a sweet, searing invasion that lasted a very long time. Beneath

the many layers of clothing she could feel her breasts
gently swell, gradually tighten.

"Why is it so simple when I'm with you?" he whispered suddenly, his cheek grazing hers, his lips nuz-
zling in her hair. "You think I haven't known other
women over the years? I've loved, Misha. But not
like this."

Her lips met his again, all hunger, all sweetness.
She thought fleetingly of his other women, and hoped
there had been thousands. Millions. She hoped he had
tried them all, every brilliant, beautiful woman who
had ever existed, and that he had found none who
made him ache as he did for her. All of her concentration was centered on inducing that darkened look
in his eyes, on matching the increased pressure of his
mouth. She heard the low, guttural sound in the back
of his throat. She could taste that sound on her tongue,
his wanting.

She drew back slowly, looking at him, unsmiling.

He bent down, picked up her hat, and brushed the
snow off it. Gradually, he fitted it on her head again,
pushing her hair beneath it.

"You are," she told him softly, "a very special
man."

His smile was lazy. He hooked an arm around her
neck, and they started walking out of the arboretum.
Matthew broke pace only long enough to brush a
single kiss near her ear. "You know I chose a walk
so I could prove beyond a shadow of a doubt that I
could keep my hands off you. Now look what happened..."

"It was your fault."

They talked nonsense the entire way home. Lorna
thought, if I breathe just right, if I don't step on any
sidewalk cracks, this isn't going to end.

It should have ended when they got back to her

place. Johnny and Brian arrived less than ten minutes later from their respective school buses, almost before Lorna had a chance to take off her coat. The boys concurred that it was absolutely essential that they build a snowman immediately. She agreed, supervising the chaos of gathering up mittens and hats and scarves, afraid to look at Matthew for fear she would see that his expression had changed with Johnny's arrival.

But it hadn't. He was chuckling, having somehow found the ingredients for hot chocolate while she was getting the kids ready to go out. When she finally closed the door on the boys, he was stirring the pot on the stove. "If I had that much energy, I'd patent it," he remarked.

She grinned. "They're exhausted after a full day in school. You should see them when they're fresh."

"I don't wake up that fresh first thing in the morning."

"Actually," she said thoughtfully, "I'll bet you do wake up fresh. Not as in wide awake, but as in hot-blooded and ready."

"Misha." He affected a schoolmaster's scold, and then chuckled when she put both palms to her flaming cheeks.

"I don't believe I said that," she groaned.

The hot chocolate was steaming. She put two mugs next to him and he poured. "You're going to Quebec with me the first of the year, right?"

"Pardon?"

"Quebec. Their winter carnival. Ice sculptures and the Château Frontenac and two weeks alone together. Can you work it?"

She closed her gaping mouth, and then opened it enough to take in a sip of scalding cocoa. Her still freezing hands curled around the cup; she decided for a minute that the cold walk had actually addled her brain. Certainly on general principles she had always been opposed to exercise. Look what the walk had done for her. All her good sense had flown out the window; her heart was convinced they didn't have a single problem to solve; and she could have sworn Matthew had just asked her to go on a two-week vacation with him.

"There's more snow due tonight," she said politely.

"Misha. I want you to come with me."

She set down the cup. There was no point in spilling the contents all over the floor. Chocolate stains were terrible to clean up. Her mind went blank. She thought, I'm getting high blood pressure already. The thudding in her chest was definitely erratic. "Matthew. I . . . Johnny . . ."

She met his eyes and was instantly drawn into a dark whirlpool. Yet the warmth in his gaze didn't quite match the sudden tension in his face, the tightness around his jaw. He leaned back against the counter, watching her. "What about Johnny?" he asked, very quietly.

"I'm not free to go away just anytime. I can't leave him—"

He nodded. "I know that. And I'll make arrangements for someone reliable to take care of him for a couple of weeks." His eyes refused to release hers, as if he could hold her gaze and propel her emotions any way he wanted. "Of course your son's important to you, Misha, but that's just the point. Let's make sure the two of us know what we're doing before we bring anyone else into it."

He was right, she thought. Rationally, she believed that, too—that the two of them needed time together before Johnny got involved, and before Richard, Sr., came into it for that matter. Two weeks alone together should tell both of them whether they were building a relationship on fantasy or reality. Her eyelashes fluttered down, and she picked up the cocoa cup again. A sudden sensation of fullness in her throat made it difficult to swallow.

The doorbell rang; it was absolutely the last thing she wanted to hear. She got up from the kitchen chair, giving Matthew one last searching glance. She knew she was going to say yes. But she wished she could tell by looking at him if he wanted an affair or a future. She didn't need a written declaration to know she would bring him more problems than she was worth in the long term. Johnny. The senior Whitaker. The past that infringed on both of them.

Once he was out of sight and she was striding down the hall, she changed her mind and decided she would have to say no to the trip. She knew that once he was near her again she would vacillate once more. You're a Ping-Pong ball, she told herself disgustedly as she opened the door.

Stan Valicheck took one look at her violent scowl and raised his eyebrows. "Have I come at a bad time? I thought we said four."

Four. Wednesday. About translating his mother's story. "Of course you haven't, Stan. I was waiting for you," Lorna lied brightly, dredging up a smile of welcome as she encouraged him to come in. She took his coat and propelled him toward her office, wondering vaguely if she could lock Stan in there and then lock Matthew in the kitchen. Not likely.

"I'll be back in two seconds," she told Stan. "Just make yourself comfortable . . ." She gave him a warm smile as he eyed her flight out the door with eyebrows raised in bewilderment.

Lorna's smile died when she left him. Pushing her hair back distractedly, she headed for the kitchen again, only to find another pair of raised eyebrows waiting for her there. "I have a client," she said unhappily. "I'm sorry, Matthew, but I'd forgotten I made an appointment for four today. It shouldn't take more than fifteen minutes..."

"I'll keep an eye out for Johnny. There's no problem, Misha."

She agreed. There wasn't any, or there shouldn't be. Yet she felt a tugging anxiety that he would make something out of her client being a man. "I'll make dinner after this, if you want to stay," she said hesitantly.

"If you end up working a long time, I'll take Johnny and go out for some fast food."

"I won't be long," she insisted.

His eyes seared hers for a second, as if dissecting her strange tension. "Go talk to your client," he advised finally.

So she did, closing the door to the office as she sat down at the desk across from Stan. It worked, closing the door. Her office and the manuscript and the brown-haired man with soft dark eyes in front of her honestly diverted her attention. She settled back, tried to relax, and once she began talking, the tensions dissolved like ice crystals in warm water.

Stan didn't even know, she realized, what the manuscript was about. Fifteen minutes slid to twenty, then to a half-hour. She had to explain the different kinds of translating problems she would encounter and the hesitation she felt in doing something of this nature. Anna would have to make the decision whether she wanted Lorna to deliver a word-for-word translation or render the story less literally but with the flavor and texture of the original. A too free translation could destroy a manuscript, change its meaning, and distort its tone, and yet word-for-word translations could do the same thing, because of the subtle nuances of language, the different idioms and mind-sets of separate cultures. "It wouldn't matter, Stan, if this were going to be something just for you and your family. But I had no idea your mother was such a literate woman. I think she's terrific; that's what I'm trying to tell you. But if she wants to sell the story—"

"I don't see that there's any problem," Stan said frankly. "Lorna, I trust you. There's no question that my mother feels the same way."

Lorna hesitated. "That's kind of you, but you hardly know me."

"We spent four hours with you last Saturday. I don't consider myself a poor judge of character. And from everything you've been saying, I would guess you'll be conscientious to a fault."

She shook her head. "All I'm suggesting is that I give the manuscript to someone else—one of the professors at the U. of M. whom my father used to know— to get his advice. Then, if he agrees with what I think, I could bring that viewpoint back to your mother."

The half-hour became a full hour before Lorna eventually stood up. Despite the success of the conference, her nerves were on edge. On the one hand, Stan was a living ego boost. He had shown the slightest hesitation at her disheveled appearance, then he gave a faint smile as if he accepted her choice of working attire. He seemed to think that everything she said was fine. Yet to be so thoroughly accepted . . . Well, it was impossible to feel uncomfortable around him, but to some extent she felt a little irritated. A man of forty should not have such faith in a total stranger, and he'd worked awfully hard to give the impression that they were friends idly mulling over a problem together, rather than two people working out a business arrangement. Finally, Lorna opened the door and ushered him out of her office.

"All right, then," Stan said easily. "You talk to your friend about the manuscript, and come to dinner on Saturday night."

"That would be fine," she agreed. Her smile radiated all the relief she felt at having coaxed him into a more professional judgment of her work. Her smile hovered, though, as she spotted Matthew and Johnny coming in the front door. Matthew was carrying a large, flat white box; the aroma of pizza wafted to Lorna's nostrils. Matthew glanced up, his eyes stopping first on her, then on Stan, and the muscle in his cheek suddenly worked like a tiny little pulse.

"I'll be looking forward to seeing you again, Lorna. Should we say seven, or would you rather make it earlier?" Stan was smiling, putting on his coat. Then he turned around as if he just realized there was someone else there. His eyes went first to Matthew and then back to Lorna.

"Stan, this is Matthew Whitaker. Matthew, Stan Valicheck. And this is Johnny." Lorna rested her hands on her son's shoulders.

Stan relaxed the moment he heard Matthew's last name. Lorna could imagine the wheels turning in his head; visiting rights for estranged fathers were common in today's society. Awkward, perhaps, but a different problem entirely than if he'd judged Matthew competition. He acknowledged Matthew with a nod, but didn't hesitate to offer a hand to Johnny. "Your mother was telling me about you. And I was telling her that we have horses. I told her you're welcome to come with her, if you think you'd like to see the stables."

"Gee, I sure would," Johnny breathed, his eyes sparkling as he silently questioned his mother.

"We may, sometime," Lorna hedged.

"Well, fine, then." Stan grabbed his coat and put his hand on the doorknob. "Seven on Saturday then, Lorna?"

"Yes."

As the door closed, Lorna pasted a brilliant smile on her face, pretended Matthew's eyes weren't boring into hers in brooding silence, and picked up the flat white box. "You brought pizza, you darlings! I haven't been this hungry in an age. Thank you, Matthew!"

CHAPTER
Eight

LORNA TOOK A small, delicate nibble of the pizza, failing to notice that a long strand of mozzarella cheese was still attached to the second pizza triangle on her plate. The gooey rope refused to break, just stretched on and on as Lorna tried to pull it free. It came loose finally, along with all the rest of the cheese on the slice. Not exactly a graceful business, eating pizza.

She swallowed and searched for a napkin. There were none. All of the napkins had been spoken for by Matthew and Johnny, both of whom were devouring their pizza slices without the slightest anxiety, while drawing diagrams of fission and fusion on their napkins. She got up and washed her hands at the sink, knowing she couldn't eat another bite.

"Got a napkin, Mom?" Johnny asked absently.

He needed the napkin to draw a rocket on, for some unknown reason. Ah, fission.

Not Lorna's forte. She leaned back against the counter drying her hands with a dish towel. Her stomach was doing cartwheels. Matthew sat there all cool and collected . . . and every word of his conversation

101

so far had been directed at Johnny.

Somewhere beneath a solid layer of nerves, anger was gradually building up in her...or was it fear? She *knew* he'd drawn the wrong conclusions about Stan. She just *knew*...

The doorbell rang. Lorna was heartily sick of the sound. Normally, no one rang the bell; Freda and Brian just walked in. Neither man nor boy looked up, and Lorna tossed the dish towel on the counter and stalked out of the kitchen. *Never,* she thought, *never* was she going to get close to another man who judged her without a trial, who became jealous and suspicious before he even gave trust a chance. He could at least have *asked* her...

You asked for it. You wanted to believe things that couldn't be true. Matthew is still a Whitaker... Her head aching abominably, she pulled open the front door, and promptly frowned. "Mr. Baker?"

Her neighbor from across the street did not make a habit of calling. In fact, they were barely on speaking terms from the time a year ago when Lorna had called the police about a raucous party at Baker's house. A little noise was fine to welcome in the New Year, but she'd been frightened; there'd been bottles thrown in the street, and the burly revelers had been knocking on doors at four in the morning.

"I'm here to talk about that brat of yours," the man said angrily, and stepped in, furiously stomping the snow from his feet.

"I beg your pardon?" She stared at him, unconsciously taking a protective step back when he put both hands on his hips. A full head taller than she was, R. A. Baker had a belly to rival Santa's, but nothing of the cheerful temperament. Brown hair bushed around his ears below a bald patch on his crown; mud-brown eyes were set close together in thick, sluggish features. Normally. At the moment, his face was florid with rage, and his eyes were almost obsidian.

"That damn kid of yours put a rock through the picture window in my living room!"

"I believe you're mistaken," Lorna said stiffly.

"The hell I am. I saw him, first thing this morning. I would have called the police then, except that I had to get to work. I *should* have called the police—"

"To begin with, Johnny didn't do any such thing. And if he had *accidentally*—"

"This was no accident, lady. And don't tell me it wasn't your kid; I saw that towhead of his, and I saw the brown coat—"

"Thousands of children have brown coats—"

"You get that kid of yours, and you get him now!"

Lorna pulled herself up to her full five feet five. The man did a fair job of looking totally intimidating, and she hated bullies. "Take a hike," she said succinctly.

His jaw dropped an inch and a half, and his cheeks turned purple. "You want me to go ahead and call the police, I sure as hell will," he said furiously. "I was willing to settle for having you pay for the window, and maybe give that hooligan of yours a good talking-to—"

"*Hooligan!*" He'd be lucky if he left the house alive.

"Misha." Matthew's hands clamped on her bristling shoulders from behind. She whirled into him, so outraged there were tears in her eyes. "This *man*—" she began furiously.

"Just tell me."

She tried, with Beer Belly interrupting every third word. If Johnny *had* accidently broken a window, he would have told her. Since he hadn't told her, she knew he hadn't done it. Johnny would never sneak into a neighbor's fenced-in yard, certainly not in the wee hours of the morning...

"And I heard you had plenty of trouble with the kid before," the neighbor slipped in.

"Not *that* kind of trouble. And as for your false accusations, *this*"—she motioned furiously to Matthew—"is my attorney. So before you—"

"Misha." Matthew's hand went to the small of her back and tugged hard at the waistband of her pants, his knuckles pressing intimately into her spine. His message, so privately delivered, could hardly fail to get through. She gathered that he wanted silence, and glanced up at him. Almost imperceptibly, he motioned toward the kitchen door, and her eyes focused on a white-faced Johnny, staring at her with sick, guilty eyes. Her heart crashed five hundred lonely feet.

"How much will it cost for a new picture window?" Matthew flatly addressed the neighbor.

"Six hundred dollars."

Lorna blanched. "But..." she started hollowly.

"Misha." Matthew turned back to the man, and released his grip on Lorna, pulling a business card from his shirt and handing it to Baker. "You have insurance?"

"Sure I got insurance. But that's not the point—"

"No," Matthew agreed bluntly, "it isn't. But then neither is coming over to vent your temper on someone half your size. I hope if felt good, because you're all through now." Matthew opened the door, not wasting any polite smiles.

"You listen here—"

"Your window will be taken care of. If you have any further problems, call the telephone number on my card. I believe we're all through talking," Matthew said pleasantly.

The other man opened his mouth and then closed

it again. "Look. I have every right to be angry."

"You have every right to be angry because your window was broken, but you have no right to be angry at the boy's mother or to take it out on her."

"If he was my kid—"

Matthew closed the door before Baker finished the sentence. Lorna was standing in white-faced silence, staring at his rigid features. She could easily read the contempt in his dark eyes, and she knew it was for her big-stomached neighbor. But was some of it for her as well? For a woman he simply assumed had been an adulteress; for a woman who raised a towhead who broke windows? *Not* how she wanted to represent herself. Nor, undoubtedly, had Matthew planned, when he invited her for a romantic interlude in Quebec, to be bogged down with the decidedly unromantic details of her life. He'd taken the man on for her, but she had a sick feeling in her stomach, and she dropped her eyes, feeling defensive and shaken up.

"Sit down, Misha."

His voice came out quiet and gentle, but she shook her head. "Where did Johnny go?"

"I'll take care of Johnny."

She shook her head again more firmly. "Of course you won't. I'll take care of—"

"Sit down."

Since her knees were caving in, she had little choice. The cushion of the chair was like a haven; she leaned back, closed her eyes, and took deep breaths. She hated men who could walk into a situation and immediately take control of it.

Matthew was gone a long time. Then, suddenly, he was bending over her, his long arms straddling her chair, his eyes unreadable as he bent to press a swift, hard kiss on her temple. When he straightened up, she studied him. He was wearing a very strange expression, a wry glimmer in his eyes, a crooked slash

to his mouth, a pervasive stiffness. "Baker was lucky
he just called Johnny a hooligan. Anything worse and
he'd probably have been on the floor with a concus-
sion. Not that you have any violent tendencies where
loyalty to your son is concerned, Misha."

She couldn't smile. "Johnny deliberately broke that
window?"

She had a glass of brandy in her hands before he
answered her. He hadn't poured any for himself. But
then, it was cherry brandy, a gift from Freda a long
time ago, and perfectly dreadful. Still, she took a sip
as he leaned back against the fireplace.

"He broke it deliberately," Matthew said. "Planned
it all just like a hardened criminal."

She gulped down a second swallow. It was that or
cry.

"Baker bought his wife a little pup a few weeks
ago. Apparently the animal wasn't trained, and messed
up in the house. Johnny saw the man beat the pup. It
didn't die, just wouldn't eat or take water or leave its
doghouse for three days. Your son watched. The wife
came home from work one day and took the pup away.
Johnny's determined to believe that she gave it away.
The boy was trying to pay Baker back."

Lorna listened in shock. "But he never told me."

"You would have believed him, Misha. But he
figured no one else would take the word of a kid over
a grown-up. And even if they did, no one was going
to punish Baker for his cruelty."

Lorna took another sip.

"Misha, stop crying."

She stared into the last of the red liquid in her
glass. "Johnny has this thing about justice. But he
can't simply take the law into his own hands and
destroy people's property. I thought he knew better.
I would *never* have guessed him capable of . . . of van-
dalism—"

She glanced up at his very sober profile, his wicked dark eyes. Just slightly, she relaxed. "Don't tell me you would have done the same thing as a kid," she accused.

"He saw a pretty little puppy crippled, all because of one man's cruelty. The dog was helpless, Misha."

And Johnny was a Whitaker, whose justice came from the heart. Still, she remembered the dreadful window that was going to cost her six hundred dollars. "I understand," she admitted unhappily, "but he has to see that violence isn't the way to right an injustice."

"Give him credit for having so much courage at nine years old. For being willing to commit himself to what he believes is right."

She set the glass down, folding her arms across her chest. Freda would have told her to land a solid ten on Johnny's backside and deprive him of his allowance for the rest of his life. Lorna knew that was one of the reasons she had searched out Matthew again; she had known he would understand Johnny. She adored her son and respected his nine-year-old ethics, but as a single parent she was also frightened of Johnny's volatile personality. "What did you say to him?" she asked suddenly.

"That I would love to see Baker behind bars. That that's why I became a lawyer, so I could put cruel people behind bars. And that by taking the situation into his own hands, Johnny didn't hurt Baker; he hurt *you*. To the tune of six hundred dollars." Matthew hesitated. "He understands now that something *he* did hurt you. And I'll pay for that window."

Her eyebrows shot up. "You certainly won't."

"I will."

"When it snows in the tropics," Lorna said politely.

He stalked forward, smiling. "I never argue with stubborn women. If you want Baker to be paid twice, Misha, you go right ahead, but in the morning he's getting six hundred dollars from me, along with a little commentary. I don't ever want to see him around here again. I intend to tell him that I'd like to rearrange his nose for him, but never mind that. Attorney talk would bore you."

"Matthew—"

But before she could say anything else, Matthew had pulled her to her feet and was maneuvering her arms around his neck. His lips were gentle on her cheeks, on her temples. His cool hands slipped under the red flannel shirt and stroked the warm skin of her back.

"Your son is waiting to talk to you, so don't start anything," he whispered.

"Me?"

"You." The graze of a whiskery cheek contrasted to the soft pressure of his mouth and she shivered. Her thighs tightened together, enclosing a secret pressure of curling desire that seemed to come out of nowhere. "I came to spend a few simple uninterrupted hours with you. Instead I find myself relegated to the kitchen while you entertain my competition."

She jumped at the opening. "Stan *isn't* competition, Matthew. He hired me to do a job."

Matthew nuzzled the soft spot just behind her ear. "Honey, I never said it was *your* fault he looks at you as if you were whipped cream. In the meantime, a quiet supper is interrupted when you try to get into a fist fight with a man twice your size, and I find myself handling your kid as if I had a right to. It's not my style to interfere where I haven't the right, Misha. Any kid without a father is vulnerable to a surrogate. No matter how sure I am, it takes two to make that decision and you're still running shaky. Scared, Misha? You think I can't see it? Put all that on top of the way you disgracefully teased me in the woods..."

"I *never* . . ."

His fingers suddenly tangled in her hair, arching her head back. His tongue brushed the softness of her lips, then stole inside to find the dark warmth. Those few inches between them suddenly weren't there anymore; his tall frame pressed closer to her, her breasts crushed to his chest, her thighs against his. Liquid suddenly seemed to flow in her veins, but it wasn't blood. It was molten gold, hot and bright, startling her with its intense rush.

"Say you're coming to Quebec with me," he murmured huskily. "I want you, Misha."

"Yes." Siberia. The South Seas. Dayton, Ohio. Wherever he wanted. She had never made a decision so easily.

Bemused, Lorna watched Matthew drive away a few minutes later. When he was out of sight, she turned toward Johnny's room and caught a quick glimpse of herself in the hall mirror. She wore the silliest smile...

Matthew almost had her believing that he initially took a distant attitude toward Johnny solely to protect the child from unconsciously becoming attached to him. He hadn't thought of Johnny in relation to Richard (or to Ron Stone?). He believed that no child belonged in a romance until the two participants knew with certainty that they were going to stay together.

Matthew almost had her believing that he hadn't jumped to any erroneous conclusions about Stan. Competition, he'd labeled the man, smiling. Wickedly smiling. She'd seen the first possessive look, had suffered an anxiety attack over dinner anticipating the kind of jealous tirade Richard would have leveled at her... Matthew had *felt* that jealousy. She would have staked her life on that.

Lorna turned away from the mirror, the smile hovering as she walked toward her son's room. Dammit, if Matthew Whitaker didn't repeatedly manage to take the wind out of her sails. She didn't know what to believe anymore. Or maybe she was still scared to believe what she really wanted to.

Johnny was curled up with his arms around his knees on the bed waiting for her with a stricken white face. "I don't like what Matthew said. I don't know who he thinks he is," her son blurted belligerently.

She sat down next to him, not touching yet. "Johnny—"

"How could he say I hurt you? I'll pay for the stupid window, Mom. You've got to understand. If you'd seen that puppy..."

She didn't have to. She saw her son's face, and she gathered him close, hugging him desperately as tears sprang to her eyes. There wouldn't be so many more times when her son was still young enough to let her hold him, to allow her to see him cry. She was shocked at his breaking that window, and she was going to be very, very tough... in the next life.

Not this one.

In this one, she fell in love with Matthew just a little bit more because he took on her son so she wouldn't have to. In the interim, there was a man in Johnny's life whom he respected, though he didn't know it yet. Johnny was very, very angry with Matthew at the moment.

"I thought he *liked* me. *Then* he says do I know what I did to my mother? Do you think I would have done something if I'd thought it would hurt you?"

"No, sweetheart," she murmured, stroking his hair. "I never thought that."

"He said he was *disappointed* that I hadn't thought about you. *Disappointed* in *me*. You never said *you* were *disappointed* in me in my whole life."

So Johnny was smarting from his first man-to-man talk. But there would be no apron strings for him.

Lorna could already see just how much a certain man's opinion meant to her son.

The delicate model airplane that Johnny had put together was a pre-World War II model, and a testimony to the patience she thought her son had. He didn't have it, actually. Lorna had decided to reglue it while he was in school, so the entire thing wouldn't fall apart. When her fingers were stickily committed to positioning the wing on the fusilage, the phone rang.

She fumbled for it, snatching up the receiver to cradle it between cheek and shoulder, becoming thoroughly exasperated when the model plane slipped from her hands. "Hello?"

"Misha? You sound ready to start throwing things."

"Not at all." She chuckled, wondering if he could read her mind. Repositioning the plane's wing, she listened to a few minutes of Matthew's chatter. He sounded tired, too tired. Nor was it like him to waste a lot of time on small talk.

"...So I'm thinking of taking him on anyway, a rookie fresh out of law school. He's got a thing for hockey, and I have tickets for the game tomorrow night...a good chance to get to know him outside an office setting, Mish, but it's been a hell of a week and I'm frankly in no mood for socializing. Will you go to the game with us? I hope to God you like hockey."

She swallowed rapidly, setting down the plane. "I love it!"

"You're sure? I hate to rope you in on such short notice—"

"I adore hockey, Matthew; it's no problem." She hesitated, wanting to scold him for sounding so tired, but she knew he would resent her noticing. Besides, it sounded wifely. "Who's playing?"

"The Red Wings and the Black Hawks."

"Wonderful," Lorna gushed enthusiastically.

A few minutes later, she set down the receiver, wrapped three rubber bands around the glued plane parts to hold them in place, and stared out the window at the falling snow. Not that many years ago, Richard Whitaker, Sr., had had a one-man attorney's office. Four more men in it now? No wonder Matthew was tired, with that kind of expanding business; she felt proud of him for his success, and she felt a modest glow of pleasure that he was willing to involve her in his professional life.

She glanced at the clock, and dialed Freda's number at work. "Freda? First of all, could you baby-sit for me tomorrow night at seven, and second, what do you know about hockey?"

"First of all, I might just be able to cancel my seven hot dates tomorrow night so I can baby-sit, and second," Freda hesitated, "I'm fairly certain that's the game that involves the puck and the hockey stick."

"I *knew* that."

"So what is it you *want* to know?" Freda added dryly. "Hockey players are the ones who always look as if they just left a dark alley at midnight and lost."

"Not helpful." Lorna sighed. "Now I assume the Red Wings are from Detroit, but where do the Black Hawks come from?"

"Toronto?" Freda suggested.

"I need a definite answer."

"Minnesota."

"If you think I'm going to continue to ask you questions at this rate—"

"I wouldn't," Freda agreed.

"Did you save last night's sports section?"

"Of course not. I use that to wrap the garbage."

"So do I," Lorna said sadly.

CHAPTER
Nine

"CHICAGO. THE BLACK HAWKS are from Chicago," Johnny said disgustedly. "And you don't go to a hockey game dressed like *that,* Mom. For Pete's sake. Don't you know anything?"

"What's wrong with this skirt?" Lorna demanded.

"Everything. It's not jeans. Hockey arenas are dirty. And cold. Like you get hot dogs without napkins," Johnny explained, as if that illustrated his point.

Actually, it did. Lorna stared at her closet. She couldn't conceive of wearing jeans to meet a potential colleague of Matthew's. Nor had Johnny ever given her a single reason in nine years to trust his judgment in clothes. She just had a terrible feeling that this was the single occasion on which she *should* trust him. He was the only one of the two of them who had ever been to a hockey game.

Deciding to follow a middle road, she took off the skirt and pulled on caramel-colored wool slacks and a silky cream blouse.

Johnny sighed. "The pants will get dirty, and you're going to freeze in that blouse."

113

"You're due next door," Lorna said sternly. She pulled on a lacy cream sweater over the blouse and looked at him.

He nodded. "Whatever happened to playing the field?"

"What field?" she asked, bewildered.

"Since when are you only seeing one guy? I thought we were going to go see those horses of what's his name."

"Stan."

"Whatever. He was nice."

And Stan had a stable of horses whereas Matthew had scolded Johnny for breaking the window. Actually, Matthew had two strikes against him in her son's eyes. A long time back, Johnny had encouraged his mother to date because he wanted a father, but it never seemed to have occurred to him at the time that such a man would have the right to touch Lorna. She understood the psychology, but it was the first time she'd walked the tightrope of putting theory into practice. It would be nice if someone would just promise her that Johnny would get past those psychological barriers and love Matthew. Because if he didn't...

"What about the horses?" Johnny asked impatiently.

"I loved horses until I was twelve," Lorna told him. "Then I finally got close to one, offered it a lump of sugar, and felt the horse bite down on my fingers so hard I thought they were broken." She walked over, pressed a kiss on her son's head, and picked up her purse. "Did you tell Brian he could sleep here tomorrow night?"

Matthew's neophyle lawyer had sandy hair, an all-American smile, and the name of Aaron Granger. His girl, Becky, was shy, clearly terrified of displeasing Matthew, and an ardent sports enthusiast. As Lorna slid into the pale gray sedan that Matthew drove on such occasions, she noted, not particularly happily, that the three of them were dressed in jeans and heavy sweaters.

Sports was obviously to be the topic of conversation, and Matthew was sadistic enough to immediately promote Lorna as an ardent hockey fan.

It was an hour's drive to the Red Wings' arena in Detroit. A week before Christmas, houses were lit up with sparkling lights; Christmas trees reflected from picture windows onto the freshly fallen snow. Shopping malls advertised the season with illuminated displays. Crass commercialism, Lorna thought idly, and loved every minute of it. Occasionally, she glanced at Matthew, who had barely had a chance to say two words to her. There were dark circles under his eyes, and a preoccupation in his expression that he was trying to pretend wasn't there. He looked remote and handsome in a thick fisherman's sweater, his dark hair brushing the collar. Intuitively, she got on his wavelength. He needed her this evening; that was a first. He wanted to know about Aaron but was honestly in no mood to play convivial host.

"And did you see that save in the last period of the Bruins game last Friday?" Aaron said from the back seat.

"I've never seen anything like it," Lorna said truthfully.

Detroit was always its own Christmas tree; its skyscrapers lit up at night like a promise against loneliness. Matthew drove farther and farther away from the lights, into the darker part of town. By the time they parked, Lorna was frankly bewildered. One carried a mace bomb or weapon in this neighborhood. She wasn't prepared.

Matthew took her hand as they walked, and never let go. She thought idly that as the senior member of

a law firm, he should really be more . . . circumspect.
Proper. They were the mature pair in the foursome.
Yet he hooked his arm around her shoulder as they
entered the arena, hugging her close. Amid the crowd,
she took the singular occasion to pat his fanny scold-
ingly. His husky chuckle made her glance around
worriedly.

The stands were steeply tiered; hot dogs were sold
without napkins, just as Johnny had warned her. The
game was just starting as they squeezed past a couple
to get to their seats. Lorna found herself between
Matthew and Aaron, and studied the oval of ice below
with deadly intensity. The whole playing area was
screened by a fence that checkerboarded her vision.

"Face-off," Becky said enthusiastically.

"Sure is!" Lorna nibbled at her hot dog, praying it
would warm her up. The place was kept at what felt
like a subzero temperature. She vowed never to doubt
her son again. Freezing, she kept her coat over her
shoulders, noted that a face-off took place in the center
of the ice, and carefully did her best to evaluate Aaron
Granger for Matthew.

Aaron was summa cum laude, University of Michigan. He and Becky planned to marry . . .

A light flashed on over the ice. The crowd stood
up and roared. Lorna did, too. "Did you believe that?"
Aaron shouted to her.

"Incredible!"

"This soon in the game!"

"Well, you know the Red Wings," Lorna suggested
brightly.

Matthew turned to stare at her. She stared just as
deliberately straight ahead, discovering their team had
made a goal. It really wasn't so hard. The goalie sat
there by the net, looking like a gorilla, lunging when
the puck came near him. The other players skated
wildly, passing around the little puck. The spectators

appeared to love every action by the home team. Their enthusiasm was catching. They stood up and screamed for everything. Probably trying to keep warm.

Keeping her eye on the ice, Lorna learned that Aaron had seen absolutely nothing of life, put Becky on a pedestal that was frighteningly high, and had gone through college on a sports scholarship. He had decided to go to law school mainly because he wanted to earn a big salary.

"Icing!" Aaron shouted, and leaped to his feet.

Lorna jumped up as well. "Did you see that icing?" she demanded to Matthew.

"Are you cold?" he whispered next to her ear.

"Certainly not," she hissed back. "I'm usually overwarm at these games; that's why I dressed this way."

"Misha—"

She glanced at him. Those dark eyes had settled on her with an intensity that caused needed heat to rush through her veins. She touched the tips of his fingers and looked away. Chaos had broken out below. One of the Detroit players was shoved into a little box, like a jail. Nobody seemed to replace him. The whole thing wasn't fair; the other team got to use all their players. Lorna, like her son, didn't like injustice.

All of a sudden, the fans were on their feet again. Lorna gulped down the last of her hot dog and jumped up.

"Did you see that assist?" Becky demanded.

"Terrific!" Lorna raved.

She screamed with pleasure like everyone else when a Black Hawks player got shoved into the jail. Then two players were in the jail. The lights flashed again. Then again.

"I haven't seen a hat trick in years," Aaron said. "This is some game."

"I haven't ever seen a hat trick," Lorna said truthfully.

Matthew pressed her hand again. She refused to look at him this time, and took away her hand. She folded her arms beneath her breasts and buried her hands under her arms. Some warmth there. The crowd's enthusiasm was catching. Loyalty was beginning to build up in Lorna. The Detroit players looked more scarred than the others.

To some extent, she was appalled. The game was simple, really, just like any other competitive sport in which one team tried to score higher than the other. The terminology, unfortunately, was like a foreign language she hadn't learned yet, but the gist was obvious. The only problem was that the players on both sides seemed to spend more time trying to kill one another than trying to score. She'd let Johnny go to a game like this with friends when she monitored every violent show on TV? And the more violent the game, the more the crowd roared its approval.

". . . So I applied to Whitaker and Laker." Aaron was responding to her questions, patiently and gently asked. "Matthew Whitaker is the best. I knew I'd be the youngest member of his firm, but I . . ."

Lorna's eyes all but popped out at the scene on the ice. She pulled at Matthew's sweater. "He *hit* our guy with the stick," she hissed furiously. "Did you see that? He *deliberately* hit him with the stick; he didn't even have the ball."

"Puck," Matthew whispered.

"Puck, then. They're letting him get away with it!"

"They're a wee bit ticked they're losing," Matthew commented. "See where they're pulling the goalie? They've got to score and now, or they're going to lose."

The goalie wasn't being "pulled" anywhere; he left the ice of his own volition, as far as Lorna could tell.

The fans hurled themselves to their feet and stayed up, screaming encouragement and insult. The puck pitched back and forth at the speed of light. Adrenaline was racing through the crowd; lights were flashing and eardrums were popping.

By the time it was over and the Red Wings had won, Lorna was exhausted, exhilarated, and without question, warm. Johnny was crazy. She could have worn a sundress.

An hour and a half later, Matthew had dropped off Aaron and Becky and was driving Lorna home. "So what was your impression of him, Misha?" he asked her.

"I have to vote no," she said simply.

He frowned in surprise. "I was almost sure you liked him."

"I did. He's a very nice young man. Bright, from a good family, ambitious, personable, nice-looking."

"Misha."

She leaned back against the car seat. "He lacks commitment, Matthew. He wants to get ahead; he's willing to work; I have no doubt he'll do his best on anything you tell him to do. But the commitment he made to go into law school was only a commitment to secure a niche in the higher income brackets. That's not a *feeling* for the law. There's no instinct there from the heart." Her cheek brushed against the car's velour upholstery as she turned to look at him. "Go ahead," she murmured. "Tell me that's a perfectly stupid way to judge a job applicant."

"Maybe that was what I wanted," he said quietly. "A perfectly emotional reaction, Mish. It was the reason I wanted you to come—to get your honest opinion." A smile played on his mouth as he turned into the driveway of her building. "There might have been another reason or two."

"Such as?"

"The way those slacks fit across your bottom." He slid up and out of the car, closing his door and striding around to her side. He opened her door, and in a moment they were strolling up the walk to her front door, his arm looped around her neck. "The way your hair looks when it's loose on your shoulders." He pressed a kiss on her hair. "The way you fill out a sweater..."

"I believe that was a sexist comment," she directed in general toward a black velvet sky.

"I take it back, about the way you fill out a sweater," he offered obligingly. At the door, he seemed in no hurry for her to produce her key. She'd understood from the beginning that there would be no long ending to the evening. It was a week night; Matthew was exhausted; it was already after midnight. Still, when she started to open her purse, he hooked both arms around her shoulders and pressed his forehead against hers. White frost-breath suddenly appeared between them. "The game was an excuse to be with you," he remarked. "And then, you happened to mention that you were a big hockey fan."

She found an imaginary piece of lint on his coat shoulder. "A good game," she said brightly.

"Have you ever seen anything like that last slap shot?" he questioned dryly.

"Shut up, Matthew."

"You'd never seen a hockey game before in your entire life."

"Maybe I just happened to want to be with you, too," she informed him gravely. Gray eyes met ebony ones. They were both smiling. "Matthew, jogging makes me ill. You might as well know it. I *hate* physical fitness. I *love* potato chips."

"What else?" he murmured.

He didn't exactly make it easy for her to find her key, insert it in the lock and turn it. He was unbuttoning her coat as she rummaged in her purse; once the key was in the lock he was pulling her close again, checking the fit of her pants with the palms of his hands, cradling her to his thighs, which were parted as he leaned against the door. Moonlight glistened down on snow, gleamed on his dark hair. His eyes shone like black opals. He was so dark in the winter's light, all tall and proud and sensual in a way she had never understood a man to be sensual. Sure of himself, but not overt about it. Experienced . . . in life, in love. He radiated that, as if he could be so sure . . .

"Have you loved many times?" she queried softly.

"Many? No." His palm brushed back her hair, first one side and then the other. "Let's get back to potato chips and the other things you think I need to know about you."

"My weaknesses?"

"I already know your strengths, Misha." Teasing kisses landed on her temple.

"I have to read before I go to sleep or I have insomnia," she confessed.

He chuckled, his arms folding loosely around her again, his fingers lifting and playing with the tendrils of hair at the nape of her neck. "Try harder," he suggested.

"I hate to be interrupted when I'm working. No human being could want to live with me the first day of my period." He kissed her, hard, on the mouth then, as if he understood how shocked she was at letting that personal detail slip out. "I like TV dinners. I lose socks in the dryer. I also lose my temper on occasion. I've always wanted to go to one of those . . . uh . . . movies. I have no control over my son, no discipline. I hate grocery shopping . . . How long do I have to go on?" she questioned. "Your turn for true confessions."

"Not yet." His slash of a smile was only token; it

did not reach his eyes. Those dark orbs held stark desire, depths of feeling where lightness suddenly didn't belong.

"I need to hear just a little more."

Was *that* why he was still lingering on her doorstep, because he thought he needed a little conversation? Lorna touched her cold fingertips to his cheek. "It's warmer inside."

He shook his head.

"Johnny's next door at Freda's."

He turned the key in the lock. The front door that invariably stuck in cold weather obligingly opened at his slightest push. Lorna had forgotten to leave a light on, and it was dark inside. Dark and warm, as Matthew was dark and warm. He took off his coat, then hers, tossed both over a chair. She barely had the chance to slip off her shoes before he reached for her.

"So you need a book to put you to sleep, do you, Misha?" She considered him brilliant for being able to follow that thread of conversation. His lips were still chilled from the outside air, until they were warmed by hers. His mouth sank into hers and stayed there as his arms enfolded her. Up and down, up and down, his hands rubbed in an evocative pattern, first very slowly and then picking up speed until the pressure was almost hurtful. Almost immediately she felt her own response start to build; then it accelerated until she felt an ache inside her that was almost painful, a longing that was alien, fierce, wild.

She could hear his breathing in the dark room, and wondered vaguely why neither of them had turned on a light. The first time they had made love it had happened the same way—so fast, like dynamite, like a raging fire from the first touch. He was so hungry for warmth, fanning those same desperate flames in herself. Her arms curled around his neck, her fingers closing on a handful of dark hair.

His leg insinuated itself between hers, his thigh tight and hard against her softer flesh. She could feel— she could almost hear—the change in his heartbeat as his hands stole beneath her sweater and blouse to the skin over her ribs. Her whole body throbbed when his palm closed over one breast, kneading the firm, swollen flesh, heating it... She felt so warm. Restlessly, she stirred, and his mouth followed hers, his tongue stealing between her teeth, thrusting and probing. She was melting like butter in the sun. She was less and less like herself; Lorna was so cautious about pursuing her sexual feelings; Lorna would never be taking such initiative, her fingers fumbling mindlessly with his sweater, angry at that heavy barrier to closeness. Eventually, he helped her remove the sweater.

"Touch," he urged her. "Touch me, Misha. I feel as if I've been separated from you for a year. As if one more minute is too much." Her palm touched the mat of hair on his chest, then curled, as she traced up and down with her fingers the swell of male breast to his throat, her thumb flicking over the flat nub of masculine nipple exactly as he was doing to her.

"Matthew..."

He slipped her sweater over her head. He undid two buttons on her blouse, then stopped to flick on the lamp by the couch, eventually undid the rest of the buttons, slowly sliding the blouse and her bra off. "God, you're beautiful."

The lamp cast a warm apricot light on her high, firm breasts, the darkened nipples pouting up for him. He looked, his touch gentle and slow as his fingertips glided over her creamy satin skin. His eyes were a dark charcoal glaze of want and the most intimate of needs.

She reached up to touch his face with the palm of her hand, and he turned to kiss her palm, then trailed butterfly kisses down her throat to the curve of her shoulder. His hands kneaded the orbs of her breasts together, and he kissed the crease between them, laving it with his tongue. She felt helpless, enthralled, spellbound; her hands wanted to clench and unclench, and her throat was scratchy. She was too warm and lethargic to move, but inside her there was nothing warm and lethargic. It was all a race, a rush, a burgeoning pressure, and a wild, uncontrollable, bittersweet longing ached through her.

His lips came back to hers and he crushed her to his chest again; she ran her hands up and down his back, all the way down to his flat buttocks that contracted when she touched, pressing his arousal between them. "Misha." He caught her hands suddenly, raising them up behind his neck. "We're not doing very well making it into the bedroom again."

"Hmmm." She didn't want to talk. So much more than the first time, she felt a sheer rush of feminine pleasure at how powerfully her touch aroused him. At how much she wanted him to want her.

"I only came in for a brief nightcap," he murmured. "You haven't offered me a single drop. We were just going to finish that little conversation we started outside."

Her lips tasted the skin at the curve of his shoulder. "You're thirsty?"

"No."

"You want to talk?"

"No."

She smiled. "You want to see the decor in my bedroom?"

"If it isn't too far."

Heavens, he was easy to please.

CHAPTER
Ten

"I'M GOING TO have to lock you up and keep you. You know that, don't you, Misha?" Matthew's palm smoothed back her mane of tangled hair. She lay stretched out beside him sleepily, her head tilted back against the pillow so she could look at him.

"I like your body, Matthew," she said absently.

He chuckled, sliding down lower on the mattress so that they were exactly face to face again. The fierce tumult of lovemaking had exhausted them both, so that they could not seem to move except in slow motion. Slow motion was fine with Lorna.

His body was beautiful. He was so lean, a long torso with small flat buttocks, ribs with no spare flesh. The curve of his shoulders and upper arms fascinated her. He had a small appendectomy scar. The long muscles in his thighs . . . everything. All of him. When he made love, his movements were fluid; he had a male grace, an animal suppleness of lithe motion and dominant control that was both fierce and lazy.

She couldn't understand what made him so different from other men in her life, what made him so beautiful to her, what made passion burst like something wild and free when he touched her. Because she loved him? But when she'd been very busy being honest with herself just the other day, she'd told herself that she was just a little too frightened to commit herself to that yet. Calling it love. Her finger absently trailed up his thigh, then turned at a right angle to touch the curling dark hair.

His hand closed over hers, shifted it. "If you don't behave yourself, I'm going to get up and fetch you a glass of wine to put you to sleep."

"I'm not going to behave myself," she told him.

He chuckled again, lurched out of bed, and disappeared into the dark hall. She was still smiling sleepily when he returned with a single glass of Pinot Noir for her from the kitchen. "This will cure your insomnia," he remarked. "We can't have you needing a book to put you to sleep every night."

"Actually, I don't think I'll have that problem tonight."

"The last thing I want to do is get up and leave you, Misha."

But he was going to. He had to; she understood that. He had to go to work in the morning, and she had one small boy who would be popping back in at seven o'clock for breakfast.

Still, he put the glass on the nightstand, shifted the covers, crawled back beside her and lifted her so that she was cradled between his thighs, her head resting against his chest. She lifted her head long enough to take a single sip of wine and then set the glass down again. Absently, his hand nestled beneath the weight of one breast, his thumb stroking, as he kissed the top of her head. "What are you doing with a single bed, lady?" he whispered.

"Twin beds are cheaper." She tilted her head back to look at him again. She liked looking at him. He had beautiful eyes. His hair was disheveled, all silvery at the sideburns. "You have a king size, I'll bet."

"Don't jump to conclusions. And no, I'm not going to tell you, Misha. You'll have to find out for yourself."

She decided she was uncomfortable and turned over so she was lying on her stomach, her breasts nestled against his chest. "Am I too heavy?" she murmured, and knew exactly why he'd shifted just a little.

"I think you know exactly what you are and what you're doing," he murmured back.

The pot calling the kettle black, she thought idly. His hands were lazily concentrating on the soft hollow at the small of her back as hers were reawakening the sensitive spot she'd discovered when her lips touched right over his heartbeat.

It was shameful, really. This wanton behavior... She didn't want him to leave. When he was with her, she felt safe in a way she had never felt safe in her life, cherished, protected, drawn into the cocoon that was Matthew's strength. She saw so many uncertainties in their relationship, so many reasons why she should want to move slowly and cautiously and sensibly, but when he was with her, her heart was full; she felt secure about the future, about love, about trust. He was the one man who seemed capable of healing all the bitter wounds from the past.

His body tensed responsively beneath her, and she slowly shifted her weight, moving her legs to make him more comfortable. His dark eyes locked with her pewter ones, which were peering out from beneath heavy lashes to assess his reaction. "So..." he whispered, his finger brushing a tender caress on her bottom lip. "This is how you want to make love this time?"

"I don't know," she whispered back, closing her eyes as she felt a dozen new little flames lick at her consciousness, reawakening a desire almost more intense than before. His touch was so exquisite. "Maybe," she breathed. "With advice?"

"The last thing you need is advice," Matthew said huskily, as he tossed the pillow from behind him on the floor. "You need nothing, Misha, to make you a more beautiful lover." He drew her down so that her hair spun a curtain around their faces, sealing them in a very private world where they could see only each other. "And I love you for that," he murmured. "But not just for that, Misha. I love you for so many reasons..."

Through half-closed lids, she watched him put on his clothes in the darkness. He had turned off the bedside lamp, but was faintly bathed in the brightness from the bathroom light. She knew he thought she was sleeping. He hadn't made a move to go until he thought she was asleep, and she understood that Matthew objected to getting out of bed and deserting her after making love, that it was not the way he wanted to treat a woman he cared for.

Yet she had only pretended to sleep, knowing he was tired and, perhaps, simply wanting to watch him as she was now doing. He pulled the heavy fisherman's sweater over his head, then absently smoothed back his ruffled hair. He cast one look at her blanketed form, at her hair spread out over the pale pillowcase, then shut off the bathroom light and walked softly from the room.

He had to put his shoes on yet, his coat. She knew he was still in the house, yet that instant of dark loneliness hit her like a bullet wound, shadowing the softer emotions that had colored her whole evening. Her eyes blinked open, and a sick feeling of dread threaded through her. Suddenly, her body tensed, and she threw off the covers and snatched up a robe. She belted the white robe as she hurried down the hall, finding Matthew just as he was putting on his coat. She approached no closer than the back of the couch by the hall, clenching the warm robe with whitened hands.

He turned, already aware of her. "I could have sworn you were asleep, you little—What's wrong?" Even in the shadows, his perceptive eyes had taken in her sudden tension.

"Nothing. Matthew . . ." Her throat was suddenly dry, yet she knew what she had to say. Already it had gone too far; already she had fallen too hard and too deeply. "We have to finish that discussion," she said lightly. He looked perplexed yet half-amused. "My faults, Matthew. Insomnia, losing socks. I have a few serious ones as well, things you should know about." She took a breath. His eyes were tender on hers as he started to take a step forward. She shook her head, and he stopped. "I've got no claims to perfection, but unfaithfulness has never been one of my faults. No, don't say anything."

She knew he'd been about to speak. His face was like granite. He looked impatient; his smile was gone.

"I know what you said, Matthew, that you understood, that it was a long time ago, that you didn't know or care now. Unfortunately, it matters too much to me. It wouldn't be so important if I hadn't started falling in love with you . . ."

"Misha."

"I was *not* unfaithful to your brother. I never slept with anyone else." She shrugged a little, trying without complete success to shake off the tremulous feeling of tearfulness, the shaky quality of her voice. "That's all. In my heart, I know we have nowhere to go if you can't take my word for truth. I could never believe you trusted me unless you know the kind of person I am. I know how it all looked; I know exactly.

But I'm asking you, Matthew; I have to ask you, and as hard as this is to say, if you can't believe me..."

Don't see me again. Don't make me fall in love any harder, any deeper. The words remained unsaid, but she knew he understood. He stood as still as a statue, staring at her, his face shrouded in darkness. "You're so damned sure I won't believe you, Misha." His voice came out low and vibrant, almost angry.

She shook her head. "I want you to...think about it. A week, Matthew. No less. Please, I..."

"All right, a week," he agreed quietly. "But then the ghosts are going to be buried, Misha. Or there just isn't a future, is there?"

That was exactly what she was too terrified to say. He said nothing else when she turned and went swiftly back down the dark hall. She hesitated before going into the bedroom, until she heard the latch of the front door. She winced at the sound, with tears in her eyes.

The horse tossed its mane and whinnied in sheer frisky pleasure at the cold day. Lorna grinned, watching Johnny astride him. The child's smile was so huge that every one of his teeth should have been cold.

"He's a fine boy, Lorna," Stan said next to her.

"The best," Lorna leaned back against the rail fence to look at Stan. Dinner was over, and it was dark out; only the yard lights made it possible for Johnny to ride the horse under Stan's watchful eye. "It was kind of you to invite him."

"No problem. I like kids. And I always feel the more exposure a young child has to a large animal, the less he's likely to be afraid as he gets older." Stan hesitated, drawing his coat collar closer around his throat. "I can't tell you how much I appreciate your doing this work for my mother. She's like a new woman, with an active interest, for a change."

"She's a darling. Two more weeks and it'll be done, Stan."

She knew what was coming and had known from the minute she'd stepped out of the car. The way Stan looked at her now, his eyes as warm as they were questioning, the slight tension in the way he'd held his shoulders... "And would you say yes if I asked you out to dinner, Lorna, when we didn't have the excuse of my mother's business?"

Lorna glanced down. "I'm afraid..." She didn't directly say no, because she had no desire to hurt a very nice man. "But thank you," she said very softly, "for asking." She could tell from the look in his eyes that he understood, that she didn't have to say any more.

A very nice, nice man. And she did not know if Matthew was going to call. She'd been condemned on the basis of strong circumstantial evidence a long time ago; and Matthew had once told her that as an attorney he set great store in circumstantial evidence. He was a believer in facts, not blind trust. She didn't expect in her heart...

But it didn't matter, as far as Stan was concerned. Another man wasn't going to soothe the heartache. If common sense told her she should keep an open mind—for Johnny's sake if not her own—her heart violently rejected the idea. Her heart, so very big, still had only room for one man.

Lorna was lying on her stomach in front of the Christmas tree in a white wool skirt and emerald crepe blouse, her stockinged feet crossed absently in the air behind her. On a sheet of newspaper in front of her were the dozens of parts that made up a Zoid. The instructions informed her that any child could easily put it together.

"If you want me to help you, Mom..." Johnny offered.

"Thank you, *no*," Lorna said crisply. *His* Zoid was done, its beady little plastic eyes gloating at her unfinished project. Santa had delivered two. Two plastic replicas of a robotic creature from a Sci-fi fantasy film that Johnny had seen three times. That alone had given it status in Johnny's eyes. It didn't do much in hers. Johnny had taken fifteen minutes to assemble his Zoid. She was on step two of nineteen.

"Look, I know you can do it, Mom. If you just take this part here—"

And she hated it when Johnny was tactful. He grinned at her, understanding her baleful gaze far too well for a nine-year-old.

"Give up, Lorna," Freda suggested from across the room.

"That would show lack of character." She frowned, snatching up the part Johnny had pointed to...once he'd gone on to the chemistry set in front of the tree.

"Honey, you've got to have the courage to admit when you're licked," Freda began, then suddenly wailed, "Brian, you're supposed to play with the presents, not the boxes!"

"I'm building a fort, Mom."

Lorna's living room was a disaster zone of tinsel, wrapping paper, bows, and boxes. The tree was a spruce, because she loved live Christmas trees, although very little of its green showed. Melted-down candies hardened in molds and strung with wire caught the open light from the windows. Quilted ornaments, decorations made of baked flour and salt and water and paint, small framed pictures, popcorn, cranberries, lights, Christmas cards...Every branch of the tree was laden with colorful decorations.

Lorna and Johnny had opened presents with Freda

and Brian on Christmas morning for the last two years.
Later, the Noonans were going to a Christmas dinner
with Freda's father, but Lorna had backed away from
the enthusiastic invitation to join them. She had bought
a six-pound turkey and all the trimmings for herself
and Johnny. Christmas had always been a lonely time
for her, particularly since her father's death, yet Johnny
went a long way toward making up for that. She'd
tried to set up their own rituals, to make it a special
day for him. Just playing and being with him, trying
out all his new toys. Caroling, a walk in the woods,
a drive to see the Christmas lights, just talking, a
special renewal of the relationship with her son...

She clicked two plastic parts together and reached
for another, glancing unobtrusively at Johnny. He was
still in pajamas, his cowlick sticking straight up, his
bright eyes engrossed in the instructions for his chemistry set. She loved that little urchin more than life.
And though she tried hard not to be overly dependent
on him, Lorna knew she needed Johnny this day.

Matthew hadn't called.

Eight days... She'd stopped expecting him to. One
part of her was never going to forgive her for bringing
up the subject to him that night, when everything had
been going so well, when she had still been in the
burst of unbelievable excitement over being with him,
just loving him, needing nothing else... *Why* had it
mattered so much? His respect and trust... the loneliness clawing at her insides certainly didn't give a
damn.

"Mom. Do you have any objection if I make some
fire water?" Johnny asked absently.

Freda groaned.

"It's like a volcano," Johnny explained, with a
careful glance at Freda. "Brian and I can do it together."

"Exactly how much *fire* is involved in fire water?" Lorna queried, picking up another plastic part and studying it from both sides.

"It says, 'will make a magical colorful flame.'"

Freda groaned again.

"Go to it," Lorna acquiesced. Johnny leaped to his feet with a beaming Brian in his wake and headed for the kitchen. Her son patted Lorna consolingly on the shoulder as he took the time to nudge his toe at part nine of her Zoid. She snatched it up, no longer proud.

While the boys were chattering in the kitchen, Freda sat down on the carpet, picking up instructions on the Zoid. "Honey, you smell like dime-store perfume."

Lorna grinned, not looking up from parts ten, eleven, and twelve. "So do you."

"I tried to talk Johnny into buying you a less... overwhelming scent."

"*I* tried to talk Brian into giving you a less... overwhelming scent."

They laughed, comfortable with each other. The boys had both presented their mothers with huge bottles of cologne, colorfully wrapped, with great pride. As far as Lorna was concerned, that made up part of the smell of Christmas. Johnny had chosen Lily of the Valley this year. Actually, she almost liked it. Last year the scent reminded her of a Detroit hooker on Twelfth Street; it might even have deterred potential customers.

Freda studied the half-assembled Zoid and handed her a part. "You can turn off that big smile for a few minutes," she said absently.

"Pardon?" Lorna glanced up.

"You've lost weight in the last week." Freda glared balefully at her. "It takes me a year to lose three pounds on a strict diet. If they ever clone people, I hope you're not on the list."

Lorna smiled absently; once, Freda's remarks would

have elicited a full-hearted chuckle at the least. "This fits. Have you got the next one?" she asked. The Zoid now had clawlike hands and looked properly ferocious; it was only missing parts of the body and legs.

"I want you and Johnny to come to dinner with us today."

Lorna glanced up again. "It's nice of you to ask us, Freda, but honestly, no thank you. We're fine here, and Christmas has always been a special time for you and your dad." She frowned. "We've covered all that."

Freda handed her another part. "You know damned well you don't really want to be alone."

"I won't be alone. I'll be with Johnny."

"You've got circles under your eyes. You're trying like hell to keep a smile on your face. You're gaunt and haggard." Freda took a quick breath.

Lorna glanced toward the kitchen, delighted at the sound of the children's laughter. "Dammit. I'll have to get a refund on that erase-circles makeup. I paid a fortune for it."

"He used you," Freda accused roughly.

Lorna sat up, snapped the thirteenth part into place, and stared at Freda. "No one," she said softly, "used me. He was perfectly wonderful to me, Freda. Don't think that. And stop *worrying*. Why on earth are you wasting all this time *worrying?*" she asked irritably. "I'm fine. Do you think I haven't coped with worse situations than this?"

Freda sat back, silent, and handed Lorna the parts to the silly Zoid. Gradually, the plastic form achieved its shape. Lorna spent all her concentration on the trivial task, and refused to think about anything else.

She had no intention of crying. It was Christmas. Holidays made some people cry. She wasn't going to be one of *those* . . .

One part of her scolded, but . . . well, there was

another part. The relationship with Matthew couldn't have gone on. Every time she bought something from a male clerk; every time she spoke with a man at a party; every time she laughed with a repairman, she would wonder if Matthew was suspicious of her. Richard would have been. Richard *had* been. She'd never been able to breathe in front of a masculine person without Richard being jealous and suspicious. She could not get involved with someone who didn't trust her. Though Matthew had said the past didn't matter to him, she would forever have walked the plank of uncertainty, would never have been able to convince him that she had never been promiscuous, that she'd had no affairs, that Johnny was of his blood—the things that mattered deeply to her. Matthew could not understand her, not in the way that counted, if he didn't understand what she had been through. Being sentenced without a trial, the desperate need she had for his trust, the fears that made up her nightmares . . .

"Mom! C'mere!"

Freda clicked her tongue as Lorna rapidly brushed away the single tear on her cheek and got to her feet.

"This is going to be a perfectly wonderful day," she told Freda.

"How I *hate* men." Freda more slowly uncoiled herself and then dropped back down on the carpet. "I'll finish this Zoid. I have a feeling you'll have more than you can handle in the kitchen."

Lorna didn't mind the chaos in the kitchen. She applauded the rainbow of smoke spouting from the paper volcano, laughed at Johnny's triumphant smile. They had raided her cupboard for baking soda, evidently a necessary ingredient for volcanoes. There was a trail of it on the floor.

Candles were flickering in the windowsills, red and green, scenting the kitchen with cinnamon and pine. More ornaments hung from her windows, hard candies that reflected the light like stained glass. The turkey was still defrosting on the counter, now surrounded by a variety of vials from Johnny's chemistry set. Some tinsel had made its way to the floor; a strand of it lay on her son's shoulder, another in Brian's hair. A second tiny Christmas tree was perched on the far corner of the kitchen table, just a foot high, decorated with ribbons and bows... Lorna had two more artificial trees in the other rooms. She'd told Johnny before he was old enough to walk that it was impossible to have enough Christmas in the house...

"Can you believe it?" Johnny demanded, looking at his lopsided volcano.

"You're a genius," Lorna agreed, ruffling his tousled hair affectionately. "In the meantime, do you think there's a chance that either of you geniuses might condescend to pick up a bit?"

"What does condescend mean?" Brian asked Johnny.

"She just means move it."

CHAPTER

Eleven

"I HAVE NO intention of leaving you with this mess," Freda said stoutly.

Lorna held up her friend's coat. "Don't be silly. It looks lots worse than it is, and the two of us have all day." She hugged Freda and then little Brian, and the Noonans scooted out the door, destined to be at least a few minutes late for their family Christmas gathering.

Lorna's smile had been bright for Freda, and it remained bright as she turned back to Johnny . . . and the disaster zone of the living room. The sea of wrapping paper and ribbons and discarded boxes was at high tide. Something to do, she insisted to herself, and in the meantime she would determinedly pull herself together and stop feeling these ridiculous waves of aching loneliness.

"The thing is," Johnny said, "to get it all located in one place."

"Exactly." Her eyebrows rose at the unexpected comment. Housekeeping had never been Johnny's métier. "It won't take us long, kiddo; then maybe we can take ourselves outside for a good long walk in the snow and a look at the Christmas lights."

As she bent over to gather up some bows, she felt something light and solid hit her backside. Pivoting, she saw a flash of color hit her in the stomach. "Johnny!"

He was bunching up wads of wrapping paper into balls and pelting her with them. Another three missiles hit her while her jaw was still gaping. "I'm just getting it all in one place, Mom. Stand still. At the same time that we get the room fixed up again, I can get my aim down just right."

"Why, you little—"

She tossed one back; that made him giggle. It had landed five feet from him in the Christmas tree. Obviously, she had to try another.

"At least *try* to hit me!"

"I *am!*"

When the doorbell rang, Lorna was laughing. Amid a bombardment of colored-paper balls and streaming ribbons, she made her way, protesting, to the door. Hurriedly, she tried to brush a cellophane ribbon out of her hair as she opened the door. Freezing air suddenly rushed into her lungs, and the brilliance of sun on snow momentarily blinded her. Not for long. She didn't need to see Matthew to know his laughter, to recognize the touch of his hand. He plucked the ribbon from her hair and leaned forward to tease her lips ever so lightly with the frosty smoothness of his own. "Merry Christmas, Misha."

For just an instant, her heart stilled. Only for a moment. The sadness haunting her eyes abruptly shimmered tremulously, trying to escape all at once in two huge tears as she threw her arms around him. "You didn't call, damn you!" she whispered. "Matthew, I..."

His eyes glinted past her, even as his arms were

drawing her close. "Merry Christmas, Johnny! I found a package under my tree this morning with your name on it . . ." Lorna would have at least drawn back slightly, suddenly aware of her son standing so still, but Matthew wouldn't let her. He cradled her close with one arm, and extended the shiny scarlet package with the other.

"Thank you," Johnny said uncertainly. But he didn't take it. "Matthew, I didn't know I was supposed to buy you a present."

"Because you weren't. This isn't even new, Johnny; I just thought you might like it."

Johnny took another look at the long, powerful arm around his mother, but resentment was clearly doing battle with simple curiosity. Slowly, he came forward and took Matthew's gift. "Can I open it?"

"I can't imagine why not."

While Johnny was very carefully removing the wrappings, Matthew took off his coat. "I missed you," he mouthed silently. His hand reached up to touch her cheek, his thumb moving slowly back and forth on her soft skin. She leaned her cheek into the cradle of his palm. As if a huge bubble had suddenly filled her soul, she felt lighthearted, champagne high. Matthew had understood her the other night. He would not have come back if he didn't believe her. She could see the love in his eyes.

"Mom . . ."

Lorna pivoted back to Johnny, who was frowning worriedly at her. "I don't think I'm supposed to take something like this," he whispered anxiously.

The scarlet paper had covered a long, rectangular wooden box, exquisitely carved. Johnny opened it, to reveal a chess set with ebony and alabaster figures. Real ebony. Real alabaster. Her son's surprise and delight were an easy read in those big dark eyes of his, but Lorna had engrained in him not to covet things that could not possibly belong to him.

"I warned you it wasn't new," Matthew said easily. He crouched down next to the boy. "I had it when I was a kid. So did my grandfather. I guarantee it's a good set to learn chess with. And I just thought maybe you might have some interest in the game . . ."

Johnny did. Immediately. Lorna watched, like a statue, the two of them together. Matthew forced no closeness, and perhaps that was why Johnny gradually forgot that moment of resentment when Matthew had first walked in. Lorna could almost hear the little wheels in her son's head turning. So Matthew was not always mean. Johnny *had* smarted over that incident with the neighbor. He was not going to commit any rash action again that he didn't think out very, very clearly . . . but he wasn't used to anyone really coming down on him hard when he misbehaved, any more than he was used to a man spending time with him.

Johnny glowed, eventually. And Lorna turned her attention back to Matthew. The gift to her son said it all. An heirloom that was passed down in the family . . . Matthew was wearing dark slacks and a cranberry wool pullover, a Christmassy shade that enhanced his dark coloring. His eyes never flickered to hers, but she knew he was aware of her. He reached for the coffee cup before she'd even set it down, tugged just for an instant at her wrist to ask her to stay next to him.

She did, with her white wool skirt tucked under her. At least she tried to keep it that way. She listened to Matthew explaining why the pawns were the most special pieces on the board, even though most of them would have to die. The queen's incredible powers; the knight's subtle ability to protect a piece. She listened to him talk about the queen and the knight and wondered vaguely how everything suddenly had a sexual connotation. She had to pull herself together, yet when she tried to get up to restore order to the drastically chaotic living room, Matthew tugged her skirt unobtrusively, and she settled back down again. She wanted to hear about queens and knights anyway. And in the meantime, she was within touching distance. Within at least smelling distance.

Matthew wrinkled his nose.

"Johnny gave me perfume for Christmas," she informed him.

"It took my whole allowance," Johnny admitted expansively.

"Johnny," Matthew said gravely, as he moved forward a pawn, "you're due an increase in allowance. You're nearly ten, aren't you?"

"In just a couple months."

"Six months." She smiled. So he liked L'Air du Temps, and not Lily of the Valley. Unfortunately, she still had to spray on more before they all got up to leave. Matthew's mouth twitched, but Johnny knew too well she always sprayed on perfume before going anywhere.

She wasn't even sure where they were going. For a drive. Matthew vaguely promised Johnny something about seeing an electric train that took up an entire basement, but she hadn't really listened. It didn't matter. What mattered was being with him. Hearing his laughter blended with Johnny's. He held her hand as they walked to the car, ignoring her son's sudden silence, ignoring again the short spell of sullenness when Lorna took the front seat next to Matthew and motioned Johnny into the back of the sedan. The mutual laughter happened again as Matthew described the pitfalls he had encountered as a child trying to put together a train while hampered by a toddler brother in diapers.

Johnny described the pitfalls of putting together a Zoid, hampered by a very pretty woman in a white skirt and a Christmas green blouse.

Lorna leaned back and relaxed as they drove. Almost as soon as she'd been aware of Johnny's possessiveness, Matthew had handled it. It would go away, she believed, as Johnny got to know Matthew better, as he grew to like him. They both were more than halfway there. Meanwhile, Matthew drove over snow-mounded roads and past Christmas lights, decorated trees in picture windows, and people dressed for the holiday, laughing in expectation of seeing their families. The university was closed, lonely. She felt inclined to pick up the small dog she saw wandering as if lost in the road. She had an urge to soothe a small child she saw crying over a broken toy through a living room window. She felt exhilarated and high; she felt she could take on anything and win.

Matthew turned down a road that seemed vaguely familiar, though Lorna couldn't quite place it. She sat up, though, giving him a curious look, wondering about his mysterious destination. She had put the tiny turkey back in the refrigerator; they didn't have to be back at any set time, but this was turning into a rather long drive. She hadn't traveled these roads in a very long time. Since . . .

He turned again, and she frowned. "Matthew?"

He reached over to cover her hand, but he didn't look at her. Lorna stared at his profile, suddenly set in very determined lines. When he glanced back to answer a question from Johnny, he managed to throw a soft look in her direction, full of love.

He turned toward the road again. Her palm, nestled in his, suddenly turned damp, and she tried to pull it away. He wouldn't let it happen, imprisoning hers that much more firmly. His fingers did the holding;

his thumb tattooed a lazy, soothing caress on the inside of her wrist.

The spiked wrought-iron gates opened when Matthew flicked a button on the console of his car.

"Wow!" Johnny breathed. "Whose house is this?"

The drive cut through five acres of snow-covered lawn. At the end of it was a three-story gray stone house, tall and imposing in the wintery landscape. Lorna felt a tight and painful lump lodge in her throat. She wrenched her hand free from Matthew's and clamped it to her side.

"It's my father's house," Matthew told Johnny easily, darting a sharp glance toward Lorna. "The house where I grew up. We've got the electric train set up in the basement, and I think you'll find my father is the perfect one to teach you to play chess."

"Okay." Johnny vaulted out of the car, full of enthusiasm and energy. Making him sit still for an hour was like trying to leash atomic energy.

Johnny closed the car door, leaving them in privacy. Lorna turned to Matthew with despairing eyes. "How *could* you do this to me?"

Those obsidian eyes of his were so soft, yet so full of steel. "Misha, I told you a long time ago that I didn't give a damn what happened between Richard and you. That happened to two other people, a century ago. The only reason I didn't call was because I knew damn well you didn't want me to until *you* were convinced I was sure. I *am* sure. I love you; I believe in you, and I don't want any more questions of that kind between us. What better time to show you than on Christmas Day; what better way to convince you than by bringing you here."

She shook her head wildly, tears stinging her eyes. "Matthew, I can't go in there. I don't want to see your father. Do you know what he called me the last time I saw him? And to bring Johnny into it! You're *cruel*," she hissed, her temper rising. "Worse than cruel, Matthew. He doesn't know—"

"And it's not going to be easy for you," Matthew agreed. He leaned over to brush the lone tear from her cheek and smooth back a strand of her hair that really didn't need smoothing. "My father knows you and Johnny are coming. I told him the way it is, Misha. He doesn't like any of it, but Misha . . ." His voice softened, though his eyes continued to have that no-give look to them. "You're still back there, worrying a long time ago. You've got to get past it. I think this really is what you want, or what you need— to bury old ghosts. To give your son and my father at least a chance to have a relationship."

She thought idly that the tone of ultimatum was familiar, even so gently delivered. She'd used it herself, when she'd told him they simply had no future if he wouldn't trust her, believe in her. He wanted the same affirmation of faith, proof that her own feelings for him weren't colored by the past. He'd tried to convey the symbolism by waiting until Christmas Day, by bringing her—and her son—here . . .

And it was true that for years she'd felt saddened by Johnny's having a grandfather he could never know. She desperately wanted Richard's son acknowledged if only for his own security, in the event something should happen to her. "But not today, Matthew," she said desperately. "Not now. I need time . . ."

He shook his head, his eyes suddenly cold. "You've had nine years. You were innocent, Misha. That's what you told me and what I believe. I trust you. But, there's a lonely old man rattling around in that house who thinks he has no grandson, when he does, and has a right to get to know the boy—has deprived himself of that right for all this time."

He put a fingertip on her lips when she tried to say something. "I *know*," he said roughly. "I know exactly how my father feels. But you're going to try. Because that's what it's going to take to put the past behind you."

Johnny thumped a gloved fist on the window, his face peering in impatiently at them. "What are you two guys doing still sitting in the car? Come on!"

As they walked up to the house, Lorna shoved her gloveless hands in her pockets and stared straight ahead, her face pale. Johnny raced ahead of them, carrying the box that held his chess set, stomping his feet in front of the two huge oak doors.

Dread was pounding so hard in her temples that she couldn't think. She stared up at the doors. No one could know what going back into this house again would cost her.

"Misha?"

She glanced at Matthew, her face as stiff and fragile as an alabaster statue.

"No one's going to hurt you," he whispered. "No one, Misha."

The long dining table could have seated thirty. The serving dishes were sterling; the hand-painted china had been handed down through generations of Whitakers; the crystal was so expensive that Johnny seemed terrified to risk taking a sip of water. A lush poinsettia perched in the center of the table, flanked by tall, flickering white candles. Carved duckling and prime rib were served and then left on the table in case anyone should want second helpings.

Lorna kept watching her son out of the corner of her eye. In part, that was easier than risking eye contact with Matthew, who had lazily and easily included her in the conversation whether she wanted that or not. Eye contact with Matthew confused her. She resented him more in those moments than she had ever resented anyone in her life. Simultaneously she also loved him more than she had ever conceived of loving anyone. Eye contact with Richard Whitaker, Sr., was out of the question. She had known exactly where she stood with him the moment she shook his hand. That left Johnny.

Her son had been struck dumb the moment they'd walked into the gracious and elegant house, a situation so rare that Lorna normally would have been amused. More than that, she was ridiculously proud of him. No, he wasn't certain which of three forks to choose, but the manners that counted were there. She felt a little like a lioness, as she casually lifted her fork to her mouth; she was prepared to protect her cub fiercely three seconds before anything could possibly threaten him.

No one had threatened him. She hadn't walked in and said, "Mr. Whitaker, this is your grandson." Mr. Whitaker hadn't countered that by saying, "He isn't, you adulteress." Richard, Sr., had directed four polite questions to Johnny, which Johnny had answered while the rest of them sipped sparkling rosé wine before being ushered in to dinner. Matthew was so good at controlling the conversation that no one really had a chance to say anything awkward.

For now, the two men were analyzing the latest crisis in the Middle East; Johnny was busy not fidgeting, and Lorna took the chance to study the man at the head of the table. Richard Whitaker was a strikingly handsome man with a head of silvery white hair and deep-set dark eyes. Nearing seventy, he looked a young fifty; his retirement had been by choice. Her former father-in-law had honest charm; and a devastating, rattlesnake tongue, both of which he could turn on and off at will. His actions sprang from an integrity that was deep-seated, unassailable, and fierce.

Richard Whitaker, Sr., judged everyone by a set of rigid standards. He either loved or hated.

Lorna took a sip of the dark red wine in the crystal goblet. She remembered well how her husband's father had loved her at first, taking her in like a beloved daughter, lavishing affection and presents and compliments on her. She remembered, just as well, how in desperation she had gone to her father-in-law when Richard had first accused her of infidelity. She had been so certain that he cared for her, so certain he would listen...He *had* listened—for five minutes. Then he had turned on her with all the venom of a hanging judge in the courtroom. He had spoken only a few concise, searing sentences about her morals and character, about how fast he wanted his son rid of her...

"Misha..."

She set down her fork and met Matthew's dark eyes across the table. Those eyes were like a lifeline. *Please*, her own eyes begged him.

You have never looked lovelier, Misha, his eyes told her. *Your chin's up, and your eyes are full of courage. Put the past behind you. For our sake.*

"While you and Dad savor an after-dinner brandy, I'll take Johnny downstairs and show him the train."

Lorna's shoulders squared as she stood up with the others. Johnny was chattering a mile a minute as Matthew laid a hand on his shoulder and ushered him to a door that led downstairs and out of sight. Her eyes trailed after them for a moment before she glanced at Mr. Whitaker.

"Would you like a brandy?" he inquired pleasantly.

"Yes. Thank you."

She knew the way through the front hall and past the living room into the sunken rectangular porch that had been converted long ago into a second living room, less formal than the first, where Mr. Whitaker always took his after-dinner drink. She descended the three steps and seated herself in a navy corduroy chair near the window. The room was all navy and gold, with tall arched windows and valuable oil paintings on the walls. The carpet was so thick it was difficult to resist taking off one's shoes. Lorna had been there many times.

Mr. Whitaker handed her a snifter of brandy and seated himself in the chair across from her. The amber liquid had already been heated, and Lorna studied the golden hue in her glass.

"The train's been a hobby of the Whitaker men for generations," he commented. "Each generation adds to it."

"I remember."

Mr. Whitaker took a sip of brandy and set down the glass. He was assessing Lorna from head to toe. She could feel it. He took in the silk-soft hair and nervous gray eyes, the Christmassy green blouse and trim-fitting white skirt. "You haven't changed, Lorna," he said, as if relinquishing any effort at small talk.

"You haven't either," she said honestly.

"I keep fit. Golf, hunting, and just walking." He paused. "Matthew tells me you work as a translator, and the boy—"

"Don't," she interrupted quietly, "say anything that will hurt my son. Not now. Not ever. I don't care what you consider to be the truth."

The gauntlet was down. Surprise flickered in his eyes first, then anger, but Lorna didn't avert her eyes from the level stare that was clearly intended to be intimidating.

"Don't you think that was a little unfair?" he suggested coldly.

"It may have been," she agreed evenly. "Where

my son is concerned, I really don't care about that."
For the first time since she had walked in the door,
she relaxed. She'd known how he felt that first instant
their eyes met, but she didn't realize how very much
she had changed over the years. She'd felt guilty simply because of being condemned a long time ago; that
guilt was gone, and so was most of the animosity
she'd harbored toward Richard's father. "I didn't want
to disturb your holiday," she said gently. "It wasn't
the day to do or say anything . . . upsetting to anyone.
I don't know what Matthew told you—"

"That he's in love with you." Mr. Whitaker took
another sip of brandy, leaned back, and crossed his
legs, regarding her from behind hooded eyes. "Matthew did not, of course, ask my opinion of the matter."

It shocked her to feel a small smile tugging at the
corner of her lips. Matthew's forte really wasn't asking anyone's opinion of anything. Mr. Whitaker evidently shared the same momentary thought, because
Lorna could have sworn a glance of understanding
passed between them.

"You're not happy," she said quietly.

He hesitated, staring absently at the landscape of
mountain and stream over the couch. "I never had
any intention of being other than cordial toward you.
Or your son." He held the brandy glass in his hands
as if they needed warming. "Matthew will go his own
way no matter what I say; he always has." He met
her eyes and held them. "We're not close. I think you
know that, Lorna. He's never agreed with certain things
I've done over the years . . . I can't really define why
the closeness isn't there, but nevertheless, he's all I
have. You think I never saw the feeling he had for
you a long time ago? He didn't even know he had it.
To fight you now, Lorna—no. And I won't fight
Matthew on anything, because I'll do nothing that

would risk losing him. I'll be seventy in a month, as you probably know." He added bitterly, "I find it thoroughly offensive for you to suggest that I would do anything to hurt your child."

Lorna looked away from him. "You turned on me, once."

"I turned on you to protect my younger son against what I felt you did to him, were doing to him." Mr. Whitaker's tone was rigid, uncompromising. "Don't tell me you don't understand that, Lorna. I can see the way you are with your own son."

"Yes." It was just a whisper. Her head suddenly ached miserably. It would be so much easier if she could see Mr. Whitaker as an enemy, but unfortunately she could understand exactly how he had felt when he had so brusquely rejected her a long time ago. She herself had so mindlessly and instantly defended Johnny on the small matter of a broken window—a minor issue next to what Mr. Whitaker had faced nearly a decade ago. "You don't want to think that Richard made a mistake," she said quietly. "I understand that, Mr. Whitaker. I know how a parent can feel...fiercely protective of a child." She hesitated, then added passionately, "But you must try to believe me, because it matters so much. Johnny *is* your grandson."

He stood abruptly and set down his brandy glass. "You've grown from a girl into a woman, haven't you, Lorna? If you want a compliment, I would even say a fine, strong woman."

Her eyes met his.

"I can respect that. And if Matthew had fallen in love with a stranger, a woman who had a child by a previous marriage, I would have been prepared to welcome them both into this house. In the same way, you are welcome here." He stared at her, his jaw rigid, those dark eyes boring into hers. "Just be very sure," he said in a low voice, "that *you* do nothing to hurt *my* son."

She realized that he was honestly prepared to go much further than she had ever dreamed of. If no trust, at least there was no animosity. He only wanted to pretend they were strangers, that was all . . . but it wasn't enough. She rose, not quite understanding why she felt all choked up and desperate. "Excuse me, would you please?" she said, but Mr. Whitaker was no longer looking at her. He was staring out the window at a crisp, snowy day. Christmas Day—a day of reconciliation. But there was no real reconciliation—no forgiveness of sins, actual or imagined—here.

CHAPTER
Twelve

LORNA'S HEELS MADE small indentations in the carpet as she hurried away from Richard Whitaker, Sr., toward the basement steps. She stopped there and put trembling fingers to her temples, deciding a quick touch-up of her makeup and hair was in order before she faced Matthew and Johnny.

Smiling brightly in the kitchen at Mrs. Harris, who had prepared such a marvelous Christmas dinner, Lorna wended her way around the table and closeted herself in the pink-tiled bathroom off the foyer. A pinched, ashen face stared back at her in the mirror. Haunted silvery eyes, huge and wild. She applied lipstick, washed her hands, brushed her hair, then washed her hands again. The repetition of the motion reminded her of Lady Macbeth and she smiled grimly to herself. She did *not* need all the perfumes of Arabia—or even a fresh dousing of Lily of the Valley—to sweeten her little hands. She was innocent of any wrongdoing, she didn't care whatever Mr. Whitaker thought. Johnny had gotten along all this time without a grandfather; he didn't need one now.

She didn't feel like crying.

Everything was fine. She understood all the subtleties of her conversation with Richard Whitaker, Sr., Master Attorney, Ret. Matthew would never guess that his father harbored any negative feelings for Lorna, because those feelings would never show. In front of Matthew. Mr. Whitaker valued his son too much. And maybe at some level he realized that his elder son had a great deal more strength and character than his younger son had possessed, that Matthew would never allow his wife to stray down the decadent path to other men's beds.

Stop it, she told her reflection in the mirror furiously. What do you care anymore? *Why* can't you just put it behind you?

She returned the makeup items to her purse. Just *be very sure* you *do nothing to hurt* my *son.* She straightened her skirt, smoothed down the front of her blouse, checked her stockings for runs, pasted a brilliant smile on her face, and unlocked the bathroom door.

She descended the steep stairs to the basement slowly. Below she could hear the chortle of Johnny's laughter and the steady hum of the electric train. Pausing at the bottom of the stairs, she leaned back against the white-painted wall and folded her arms. Her head was aching and her heart was still beating in a terrible, painful rhythm that she refused to define; yet she could not help relaxing a little at the sight that greeted her.

Matthew was on his hands and knees, as was Johnny; their rear ends faced her. The train was more than a few decades old; the engine was a good foot long and made all kinds of authentic old-time noises. The tracks led from the huge main storage room of the basement through the laundry rooms and pantries, and back to the game room where she was standing

now. It had to have taken Matthew days to set it up.
Tunnels and crisscrossed tracks and flashing lights,
makeshift hills and valleys and switchyards...She
shook her head, debating who was the happier child
of the two.

Matthew moved and caught sight of her. She decided abruptly that she was mistaken to label him a
child. His dark eyes seared hers, assessing so per-
ceptively that she felt stripped and laid bare; she saw
a flash of anger in those depths, and knew she had to
do a better job of covering up her emotions. She would
not be responsible for a rift between father and son,
nor could she blame Mr. Whitaker for her own desperately unhappy mood.

"Misha."

She smiled brightly, stepped over the track, and
crouched between the two of them. "I don't believe
this!" she said enthusiastically, eyes thanking him for
the trouble he had gone to for Johnny.

"Mom! This thing can go a zillion miles an hour.
Just watch!"

She watched. It seemed to run smoothly at a million
mph, but cracked up in a terrible pile at a zillion.
Johnny burst into chuckles, and crawled along the
floor on his knees to fix it. "On the curves, you have
to go a little slower," he explained.

"I don't suppose you'd let a female run it," Lorna
wondered idly.

Johnny's head was down. "Some females, yes.
You, no."

"Johnny!"

Johnny's eyes darted up at Matthew's stern ad-
monition. "You just don't know her that well. You
can't let Mom near things like this," he explained. "I
wasn't being fresh, Matthew."

"I do believe we can allow her one turn at the

controls, even if she isn't particularly mechanical," Matthew said dryly.

Johnny shook his head and shrugged. "It's your train." He brought the controls over to his mother and explained in nauseatingly exact detail what to do. If Matthew hadn't been biting his lip to keep from laughing, Lorna might have been tempted to rearrange her adorable son's nose. She started the train by pulling the lever, and watched it zoom and curve until it was out of sight. It was chugging along perfectly, tooting and smoking at interesting intervals, switching and backing up...until her heel caught on one of the electric wires and all the lights went out.

When they went on again, she saw that Matthew had put his head in his hands. Johnny looked only at Matthew. "I'm not going to say I told you so because you're a grown-up," Johnny informed Matthew. "I have better manners than that."

"Let's take her home," Matthew suggested.

"Couldn't you just send her back upstairs again? She can talk to Mr. Whitaker."

Matthew stole another glance at Lorna. She thought she'd had him fooled, because she knew her own laughter had been real in those few short minutes. There had been honest pleasure just in being with both of them. Yet Matthew continued to stare intently at her, and seemed to see beyond her smile and the banter with her son. "It's getting late," he insisted quietly to Johnny. "I guarantee you can come back and see this another day."

By the time they got home, Johnny and Matthew were hungry again. It was dark, and Lorna put out some of the feast she'd intended to serve for Christmas dinner for herself and her son. Lopsided Christmas cookies, gaily decorated; a green molded salad with cherries and tiny candies inside; dips with crackers and fresh vegetables . . . It was not exactly a nutritious snack. Certainly not served with sparkling Burgundy and Johnny's Boston Cooler.

Her towheaded urchin, never one to let a subject die a natural death, brought the two Zoids to the kitchen table. His own lurched and threatened in terrible menace from its four-inch height, while hers fell over with every third step. Matthew just looked at her.

"There are many, *many* men who aren't in the least mechanical," she informed both of them.

"He's only nine years old," Matthew reminded her.

Johnny had a few more choice bits of information to impart before Lorna finally got him to bed, kissed him seven times, hugged him for a while, and left him to his almost-ten male-chauvinist solitude.

By the time she returned to the living room, Matthew had lit a fire in the fireplace, pushed most of the debris behind a chair, and removed his sweater; he was reclining, shoes off, on the couch. "Come over here," he suggested, patting the inch and a half of empty space next to him.

She smiled, curling at the bottom of the couch instead with her feet tucked up under her. "For some unknown reason, I'm so tired I can hardly move," she admitted.

He nudged her calf with his foot, and when she failed to respond simply sat up and took her back down with him, not content until her head was tucked into the crook of his shoulder and her legs were captured beneath one of his. She couldn't move. She had the feeling that was exactly what Matthew had intended, that he had watched her exhibition of restless energy since they had come back from his father's and correctly interpreted all of it.

With his hand on her hip, he kissed the crown of

her chestnut hair. "I think you're wine-tired," he whispered teasingly. "Two glasses, Misha. You're quite a drinker."

"Don't *you* start."

"Johnny tells me that you can swear in several languages. Can you?"

"I have never sworn in front of that child in my entire life."

"Except in German. And Russian."

Lorna sighed, curling closer to him, rubbing her cheek against the soft white shirt fabric near his shoulder. "What else did the little monster tell you?" she murmured dryly.

"We don't much like men who touch our mother, now, do we? And we're more than capable of taking care of you all on our own. We like *friends* to take us *both* out on outings. For example, hockey games. Seeing toy trains. *Maybe* tobogganing..." Matthew sighed. "I didn't touch you throughout dinner, did I? Not even when we were downstairs together. I can't imagine why I like the little imp. I know darn well he's waging war." A wry smile touched Matthew's features, but his eyes told her he was serious. "It *is* a war, Misha, but not to worry. It will just take some time to convince him he can't lose for winning. I'll be patient."

She thought fleetingly how typical that was of Matthew, to let her know he understood Johnny's possessive instincts, and by treating the subject lightly to also let her know that she could trust his handling of it.

He seemed to handle a great many things well. Her temples, for instance, where a headache raged tense and tight; his thumb rubbed caressingly back and forth, soothing away the pain she had never even mentioned to him. And her lips, for another. When his mouth sank deliciously on hers, she felt something give inside her that had been knotted up for hours. Feelings of hopelessness and helplessness, a residue from the past she thought she'd managed to get rid of; the wounds that had seared open again after her encounter with his father.

Her hands rippled through his hair, and her aching breasts nuzzled deliberately against his chest as she curled closer to him. He tasted so sweet; she wanted to lose herself in that sweetness. Before, she had forgotten everything else when he touched her; she courted that kind of explosive passion now, her hands rippling down his shoulders and arms, then to the front of his shirt, suddenly in a desperate hurry to get past buttons.

Buttons? To get past pain, past thought, past this strange aching ball of hurt inside her that refused to ease. She wanted to love Matthew, to promise him that she would never make him suffer, to wrap him up in silk arms and satin smoothness. She could feel his dark, soft eyes watching her, and paid no attention. Her already turbulent emotions had been set on a roller coaster. There was no getting off. She felt panic at the thought of getting off. She needed Matthew so badly, now, this minute, instantly, an hour ago . . .

Her lips pressed fierce kisses on his throat, down into the furred mat on his bare chest. Her leg curled between both of his, firing his arousal. In some other world she felt his hands smoothing back her silky hair, his feather-light kisses trying to soothe. She didn't want to be soothed. She kneaded the flesh of his back, willing every other thought to fade in her head, willing that drumbeat of desire to flood her ears, block out everything but Matthew. It could happen; she knew it could. She felt his body respond to her, his muscles tightening in promise, his skin taking on warmth, his breath shortening. Yet when her hands reached for his belt buckle, she found her fingers stolen by his, her arms placed around his neck.

His mouth reached for hers, in a single dominating kiss meant to stop her frantic movements. It did. He cradled her head in his palms to touch her lips again, his dark eyes gentle on hers. "Stop crying," he whispered. His thumbs lightly brushed away the moisture beneath her eyes that she hadn't even known was there.

"I want you to make love to me," she whispered back fiercely.

"Do you?" He pulled her close, once more raining kisses on her closed eyes, on her cheeks, on her temples. For no reason at all, she was suddenly trembling all over, gasping to keep from crying. "Dammit. Tell me, Misha."

She shook her head.

"Tell me," he insisted beseechingly.

She closed her eyes painfully, feeling more vulnerable than spun glass. "I'm sorry. I..."

"Just tell me."

With her head still cradled in the crook of his shoulder, Matthew shifted both of them, so that by the time she'd brushed away those few mortifying tears she was cradled on his lap and held in a protective cocoon. Or were those arms steel bars? Because he was not letting her get away.

"He wasn't in any way... unkind, Matthew," she said miserably, needing to reassure him immediately of that. There was no reason for either of them to say Mr. Whitaker's name out loud; they both knew what was wrong. "I never expected him to believe me about Johnny, anyway. I never even expected he would be as... civil as he was. It was just..."

"It was just that you wanted him to acknowledge his grandson," Matthew said softly. "Or did you, very badly, want to hear from him that he just might have been very wrong about you, Misha? Can you dare acknowledge such feelings?"

"I . . ." She took a breath, then another, her whole body still violently shaking. "You just don't know . . . what it was like. Being condemned without a trial. Without even a *hearing*. Feeling judged, feeling guilty and ashamed when it wasn't like that . . . I went to see him back then, to ask him for help, and he treated me with such contempt . . ."

The words spilled out, one after another. Words she had never spoken out loud before, feelings she had never expressed. What Ron Stone had really been like, her inability to cope with the situation at the time, that awful afternoon, Richard's reaction, then his father not even making the attempt to listen . . .

"But I would have listened, Misha," Matthew scolded fiercely. "I *tried* to talk with you. You shut me out. Why couldn't you let me help you?"

"Because . . ." But she didn't know why. She had been ashamed at the time, embarrassed, mortified, proud. Because Matthew had controlled a strange little corner of her life, even then. His respect had always mattered. All of it. None of it. She didn't know why.

"It doesn't matter anymore," he murmured, and held her close until the need to cry eased and she laid her cheek against his shoulder. "There's more, I think, Misha. There's more that you have to let go of. But not now. Not now," he repeated, brushing his fingers through her hair over and over. "Just let it be with my father," he murmured gently. "It will happen, sweet, about Johnny. If you want to know the truth, I think my father knows already that Johnny is Richard's son. I watched him when he first set eyes on the boy . . . I see the Whitaker in Johnny more and more, and my father isn't obtuse, either. He simply finds it hard to admit that he could conceivably make a mistake. My brother never could admit such a thing."

She heard the slight trace of bitterness in his voice. Lorna looked up at him, wanting to respond, but he gave her no chance. Kissing her gently on the forehead, he stood up and set her on her feet, pausing long enough to hug her close yet again. "I don't want you worrying about it anymore. You, Misha," he whispered, "*you* matter. When you're troubled, tell me about it. You had to bridge that silence with my father alone, but that's done now. The rest we can handle together. Make no mistake about one thing: you're not going to elude me, love. I want you, all of you... I love you, more than those three words can express..."

She looked up into his eyes. He was so sure, so absolutely sure; she saw love, strong and determined, and possession. A love so deep it almost frightened her. He wanted her; he loved her. *She* was the one who had erected barriers, which he seemed to understand more than she did herself. And if she wasn't going to work on pulling down those fences herself, he would force her into action, so he could have what he wanted.

Had she ever really thought he might only want an affair? This man wanted to possess, body and soul.

When she awoke in the morning, she sensed that something was different. Before Lorna even opened her eyes, she tested out that feeling. Early morning brightness came in the appropriate window; she recognized the faint, familiar scent of Johnny's gift cologne, and the kind of silence that existed only in the morning before her son was awake. The room was on the cold side, exactly the way she liked to sleep, the comforter tucked around her just so. Absently frowning, she readjusted her pillow and closed her eyes again for one more tiny catnap.

Something hard and small brushed her cheek. She was thinking of Matthew. He'd put her to bed last night because she was exhausted, only by then she

hadn't been exhausted. Nor had she wanted to be
separated from him. He was a bewilderingly complex
man. He'd stopped her from making love so they
could talk, but they'd stopped talking just as abruptly
so he could make love to her . . . a slow, lazy seduction
that began on the way to the bedroom. His caresses
had been deliberately arousing, leaving her sleepy and
wanting him and loving him. It had slipped out then,
so naturally. "I adore you, Matthew. I never thought
I could love as I love you . . ."

Those beautiful brooding eyes had captured hers.
"That's all I've been waiting for, Misha . . ."

But they *hadn't* made love. He had left. It made
no sense . . . She stirred again, and felt an odd, sharp
little scrape on her cheek. Grudgingly opening her
eyes, she squinted down at the offending object, and
her heart stilled as she stared at her finger.

There *was* something different this morning. A ring.
She wore no rings to commemorate her commitment
to Richard. Certainly not a single brilliant marquise
diamond, set exquisitely in antique gold. Certainly
not on *that* finger. But she wore it now . . .

"Let's see it once more," Freda insisted.

The mall was packed with throngs of tired people
returning presents and hustling toward the after-
Christmas sales. It just wasn't that easy to stop every
five minutes, readjust all the packages, and find enough
space so they could both stare at the ring again.

"It's probably the most beautiful ring I've ever seen
in my life," Lorna said absently.

"I'm not sure we need to go *that* far. Mrs. Van-
asterbilt—" Freda began.

"Should have such taste."

"You're probably right."

They picked up next year's wrapping paper and
bows, exchanged Johnny's sweater for a larger size,

Brian's boots for a smaller size; both bought night-gowns on sale and debated whether to risk looking into the dress sales even though neither of them wanted to spend any more money. Useless friend that Freda was, she talked Lorna into buying a lavender sweater and a lavender and pale blue plaid skirt, then didn't buy a thing herself.

"That burnt orange would have been perfectly beautiful on you," Lorna scolded, as they stood in line for a seat in the coffee shop.

"Not my style." Finally, they were ushered to a booth and piled their packages next to them with mutual weary sighs.

"It was, too. Freda, you have a very nice figure. And the color would have been special on you," Lorna told her as their waitress brought coffee.

"I need to lose weight." Freda pushed off her coat and crossed her arms on the table. Lorna grinned at her friend's navy sweatshirt. "There are only two things wrong with men," it said, "everything they say and everything they do."

"Let's see it again."

Lorna obligingly put her hand on the table.

"Offhand, I'd certainly say he made up for forgetting to give you a present yesterday," Freda remarked dryly, and then gave Lorna a basilisk stare. "I don't know what's brighter. That stone, or your eyes. You have no idea how annoying it is to sit across from someone in love."

"Will it help if I pay for the coffee?" Lorna asked.

"A little." Freda shook her head ruefully as she stirred her brew. "I could see it coming. You were either higher than a kite or moping around like a dead sponge. Washing your floor three times last week..." She leaned back, bringing her coffee cup to her lips. "I could have sworn the last I heard you weren't even thinking about getting married again."

"I wasn't," Lorna said absently.

"You're being awfully closemouthed about how he staged the whole romantic scene. When did he ask you to marry him?"

"I adore him, Freda." Lorna's tone was grave as she changed the subject and abruptly put an end to Freda's affectionate teasing.

They talked about clothes, bills, jobs, and cats. They were still talking as they drove home, stopping to pick up the boys from a playmate's house along the way. The roads were a potpourri of slush and traffic; Freda kept chattering, and the boys in the back were bickering at high speed.

Lorna had her hands on the steering wheel at ten and four, a position where the ring could continually wink brilliantly at her. Like a silent beacon, the diamond on her left hand gave her messages only she could hear. Matthew loved her.

Pausing at a red light, Lorna touched the marquise diamond, well aware that in fact there had been no proposal; the candlelight seduction Freda had assumed had never happened. He had simply left the ring on the appropriate finger for her to find, and he had left her in silence to think on it, because Matthew was unforgivably, cruelly, disgustingly fair.

The light turned green, and she put her foot on the accelerator. He had hedged his bet, more than a little, by arousing her until the only thing on her mind when she went to sleep was her greedy, aching soul, avid for the kind of fulfilment only he could give her.

He was very good at setting up all the stakes on his side, she thought ruefully, a small, dreamy smile playing on her mouth. He hadn't just promised her trust; he'd given it, freely, in teasing her about Stan, in believing in her when she'd needed to be believed. He'd respected her feelings for her son; he had put her feelings ahead of those of his father; Lorna knew well he had told Mr. Whitaker straight out that she came first in Matthew's life. He was a man she could trust, a man of compassion and strength and sensitivity. A man of the sort she'd never believed had existed. And when he touched her . . .

Such love . . . All that morning she'd been exhilarated, restless, giddy, laughing at nothing, not able to think a single coherent thought. She adored him; she needed him; she wanted him . . .

So why, she thought idly, did she feel so scared?

The ring winked at her again as she made a left turn. She *knew* why he'd given it to her exactly the way he had. No soft lights and intoxicating seduction. He'd wanted a commitment from the soul, a clear-cut, honest decision that came from love. *We've tackled Johnny and my father and your feelings about the past, Misha. You were wary when we first met. I don't want the shadows. I want it to be you and me alone, and I want you to be damned sure.*

It was amazing, what an inanimate ring could say.

"Mom," Johnny said patiently, "how many times are you going to keep circling the block?"

She glanced at her son in the rearview mirror. "One more time. Anything wrong with that?" She couldn't afford to believe there was a jinx on a second time around.

CHAPTER

Thirteen

". . . FLIGHT THREE-OH-THREE to Toronto and Montreal now boarding at gate three-oh-seven. All passengers . . ."

"Misha?"

Lorna's head jerked up as Matthew touched her arm, her hand nearly knocking over the coffee cup as she hurriedly stood up. Her nervous clumsiness embarrassed her; she flushed as she said brightly, "Finally! I was beginning to think they were going to ground the plane because of snow."

"They wouldn't dare."

Lorna raised teasing eyebrows as she snatched up her purse. "You mean you wouldn't let them. I know exactly what's on your mind, Mr. Whitaker."

"So do I." He linked a protective arm through hers after dropping a bill on the table, and they worked their way through the crowded airport. "And I would like to tell you in exact detail what else I have on my mind when I have you completely alone." The low, husky drawl was whispered in her ear, just as if there weren't a thousand people all around them.

Lorna shivered, a response she could no more have controlled than she could control her breathing. They had waited more than an hour for their flight to Quebec. Metropolitan International Airport was filled with people who had waited hours for flights delayed because of the blizzard outside.

The walk to their boarding gate would have been lengthy on roller skates. As it was, no one seemed inclined to move willingly to get out of their way. Fractious children with hot red faces were tired of wearing heavy coats and holding their belongings and sitting still. Their mothers, once dressed and coiffed and made up for travel, had wilted. Businessmen swung briefcases like lethal weapons, and the confusion of noise was incredible. The airport loudspeaker was paging particular individuals to remove themselves from the list of lost persons, to pick up their tickets, to answer a summons to speak to someone. Trolleys were clattering through the terminal, laden with luggage; adults were chattering at fevered pitches and babies were crying.

Lorna felt like a pincushion with too many pins piercing her all at once, which was undoubtedly why her pulse kept beating in this strange, fluttery rhythm. Her hands were atypically clammy. For a short time, in the quiet of the small coffee shop, she even wondered if she was coming down with a fever. Her stomach was churning; her legs felt shaky . . .

She knew none of it showed. Matthew's eyes would have picked it up if she hadn't looked well, and when she'd looked in the mirror at home before leaving for the airport, it had told her that for some strange reason, she almost looked beautiful. Bone-colored pumps complemented good-looking legs. Her traveling suit was burnt orange, a favorite color, the wool skirt clinging very nicely to her slim hips; she'd eaten cottage-cheese lunches for a week so that she could afford to buy the cream-colored silk blouse that was so flattering. Her chestnut hair had a gloss like sun glow; her eyes had been subtly, alluringly made up...A healthy, lovely woman had stared at her from the mirror that morning. A woman who loved, a woman who looked loved.

Don't hurt him, Mr. Whitaker had warned her.

"Misha—" Matthew clutched her shoulder, weaving her out of the way of a man in an airport uniform racing down the corridor. She hadn't even seen him.

There *was* something wrong with her. Adrenaline was speeding through her veins; her stomach was cramping; she felt the strangest feeling of dread hammering in her temples. She was reminded of her college days, waiting for the test to be passed out in Chemistry 101; it was like the day she had taken Johnny to the emergency room with a bump on his head and they had insisted she stay out in the waiting room. She didn't even notice the man in the red sports coat eye her up and down suggestively, nor did she see Matthew icily outstare him until the stranger flushed and turned away. A child raced past her; she barely felt the jolt.

Finally, they reached the last turn of the long corridor. A few hundred feet ahead was the small cubbyhole where a stewardess was checking tickets. After this automatic procedure, they would be in Quebec in a few hours, just the two of them at the Château Frontenac. Fourteen days of sheer-luxury vacation. A honeymoon ahead of time? she had joked to Matthew. He informed her that they needed at least that much time anyway. One week in a cold climate, one week in a hot. To see which they liked best. And if they needed to test out any other temperatures that suited her fancy...

"Wait here, Misha. You don't have to join that madhouse yet..."

She watched the man she loved more than life detach himself from her and join the rest of the throng of humanity trying to bully the stewardess into letting them go first. Matthew was different. She wasn't in the least biased. He was simply without question the most handsome man there, but it wasn't just that. It was that shock of dark hair on his forehead, and those grave dark eyes. His quietness, a total control and assurance that set him apart. The character lines around his eyes, the way his shoulders fit a suit.

A brown-eyed blonde kept looking at him. Lorna stepped ahead just a little, blocking the woman's view. He was handing the tickets to the stewardess. She said something. He chuckled in return, his heart-stopping mouth slashing in a smile, and the stewardess's eyes lit up. He had relaxed her in the frazzle of confusion; that was his way. Almost instantly, he was looking up again, searching the crowd for Lorna.

She saw the grave look in his eyes when he didn't immediately spot her, though she had only moved a few feet. She saw that special light immediately go out of his eyes, and her hands started trembling. *Just be very sure that* you *do nothing to hurt* my *son*. Why couldn't she get the damn sentence out of her mind?

The crowd started boarding, all in a rush. His eyes captured hers. Captured, held, scolded her for moving, rejoiced that he had found her, and . . . loved her. He motioned, but she suddenly couldn't move. For some insane reason, there were tears in her eyes, and a lump so thick in the back of her throat that she couldn't breathe.

"Misha?" This time it was Matthew who bumped into people without noticing. Concern etched sharp lines around his eyes as he hurried toward her, his hand instinctively reaching up to touch her cheek. "Darling, what's wrong? We've only got another minute to get on—"

"I can't marry you, Matthew. I'm sorry. I can't go on that plane. I can't. I...can't..." It was all in desperate, choked whispers. Not because of the crowd. She didn't even see the crowd. She only saw Matthew's face. The smile set suddenly in steel, shock, bewilderment, the haunting chill of stark pain, that special loving light in his eyes dimmed.

"Misha. If it's leaving Johnny, you know he fell in love with Mr. Rudowsky. And Freda's just next door..." She could tell that he knew it wasn't anything to do with Johnny. She'd never seen a man's face go totally ashen, and her heart lurched. Splintered. "You don't mean it, dammit. Misha. I *love* you. I know damn well you love me."

"Last call for flight three-oh-three to Toronto and Montreal."

"I love you, Matthew. But I can't marry you. I won't. It's just...wrong. I should have known—"

Matthew cast a distraught glance at the stewardess, who was motioning them toward the plane. It was past time. The cubbyhole of a lobby had emptied of everyone else. There were only the two of them. And a plane that wouldn't wait. Matthew grasped her shoulders and tugged. "Dammit. You're coming on that plane with me. We'll talk there. This is no time—"

"No," she said desperately. "Matthew. I mean it. I'm not going."

"Mr. Whitaker, I'm sorry, but—"

He motioned the pretty stewardess away, his eyes never leaving Lorna's. Boring into hers. "I'm going to marry you, Misha."

She shook her head wildly. "Go," she whispered. "You were planning on this vacation anyway, Matthew. Take it. Get away. You'll see I'm right."

She couldn't stand the look in his eyes any longer. She couldn't stand herself. When she glimpsed the small sign for the women's room across the hall, she headed toward it. She heard his shout, but she had already taken off at a run.

The heel of her hand jammed against the door and just that quickly she was through. Inside, away from him. She leaned back against the white-tiled wall, gasping, aching for breath.

Through eyes blurred by tears, she suddenly realized there was a woman gaping at her. She was not alone in the rest room. The other woman was older, with a sparkle of white hair shining with a blue rinse; she was dressed all in powder blue. "You just have to leave a loved one behind, too, honey?"

"I . . ." Lorna saw that the other woman, too, had tears in her eyes. "Yes." *Go away, please.*

The lady talked. How hard it was to let her husband get on the plane, how she hated separations. Lorna didn't hear. She wrenched herself away from the wall and pretended to get a brush and lipstick out of her purse. Tears kept flowing out of her eyes. Big, fat tears, agonizingly slow. They wouldn't stop. She pretended she could see herself in the mirror and applied powder over the tears, which didn't have any effect at all. The woman finally left, and Lorna stopped trying.

She leaned both hands on the sink and closed her eyes, willing herself not to be sick, waiting for the flood of tears to cease, terrified they were never going to. A thousand things flashed through her mind. She could not walk through the airport crying hysterically. She had no way to get home. She had no desire to go home. There was nowhere to go. Her reading glasses were on the way to Quebec. She had no tissues. When she traveled with Johnny, she never forgot tissues. For herself, she never considered that she would have to mop up the Great Salt Lake. Could anyone actually die of heartache? Her whole body was shaking violently . . .

Don't hurt him, Mr. Whitaker had charged her.

Nine years flashed in front of her mind in seconds. The guilt that had been so much a part of her life. The fact that she had been wrongly accused of adultery had shaped so much of those years. She had never trusted another man until Matthew. She had chased away any hint of commitment on the part of any man who had dared try. *Never again* was she going to put herself in a position where she could be tried and judged without a sentence.

She knew all that. She couldn't imagine how she had successfully lied to herself for so long.

Guilt was the key. Feeling guilty, when she had convinced herself she was innocent. Only Matthew had loved her, and she had fallen in love with him, facing up to the real truth. She had felt guilty over Richard, because she *was* guilty.

Not of adultery. But in her own heart, of worse. She had pledged to love, honor, and cherish Richard for the rest of her life, and she had been very, very sure she was doing the right thing. But less than a year later, she was out of love. Less than a year later, she cared very little for him, could not seem to love, to respect, to cherish him. Richard had never done anything terrible to her, yet she had hated it when he so much as touched her . . .

And for nine years, she had buried those feelings, refused to admit that she was incapable of lasting love. Getting a man's love, yes. But holding it, loving for the long term . . . No one could have made more of a mess of her life than she had nine years ago. And now she loved Matthew just too damned much . . .

Her eyes were on fire. Mindlessly, she plucked paper towels from the dispenser, soaked them in cold water, and held them against her eyes, leaning over the sink. The most horrible sounds were coming from her throat. She was terrified someone was going to walk in. If she pressed the heels of her hands into her eyes, she would stop crying.

"That's enough, Misha."

She jerked up, shocked. Matthew could not conceivably be in the women's rest room. Yet he took the matted paper towels out of her hands, brushed them one more time against her eyes, then pressed her face to his shoulder and folded his arms around her like a vise.

"No more," he said furiously. "Dammit, Misha, you'll make yourself sick crying like that. Stop it. Right now."

"Matthew..." She could smell the soap he used, the unique smell that was Matthew. His whole body was rigidly tense; his shoulders wouldn't give... but the fingers that brushed back her hair were infinitely gentle. He cupped her face in his hands and forced her to look at him through tear-blurred eyes.

"Why do you judge yourself so damned harshly for being human, Misha? So the long term is scary as hell. You and I are going to make it. We're going to laugh through the good times and fight through the bad times, and we're going to make it work, Misha. Because what we have is worth fighting for."

He searched through her purse. He knew nothing about putting powder on cheeks, nothing about hairstyles. She could tell by the way he used a brush.

"Matthew—"

"You think you're the only one who's ever had a failure in the past, Misha. You're the only one who passed sentence on yourself, honey; no one else has. No one else could. We're all in the same boat. All people... trying hard. You want a promise, Misha? All right, then. I promise that you're going to love me until you're ninety-four and I'm a hundred and thirteen. And you are *never* again, *never*, going to cause me to hold up a plane with two hundred and seventy-four people aboard. I mean that."

She glanced up. He *was* furious. Not unsure, not less loving, not less compassionate, but almost angry enough to shake her. Something jelled inside her. All the pain that had ached through her... No, it wasn't simply going to go away. But love was bursting inside her, completely different from what she'd once thought love felt like. It really wasn't the same; she had been very stupid to think she was the same young girl she had once been. And suddenly she found it impossible to believe that she wouldn't love Matthew when she was ninety-four.

"Ready?" he demanded harshly.

"Ready," she agreed. All her love was in her eyes. And suddenly laughter, too—to match his.

One arm plunged into the deep, sudsy water. Lorna felt fingertips marching down her thighs, over her knees and calves. Finally, they lingered on her toes, and Matthew's arm came up dripping. "Still cold," he pronounced.

"Matthew, this water is at cauldron temperature."

"Your toes were cold."

Lorna gave in and sank farther down into the luxurious warmth, leaning her turbaned head back against the porcelain tub. Matthew was perched on the edge, wearing a huge white towel, alternately sipping Caribou, a drink that was popular among the Québecois, and checking her body temperature. Since she warmed spontaneously to his touch, there had really been no need for a bath at all, even if they had spent most of the day in subzero temperatures; but there was no telling Matthew that. He was not in a reasonable mood.

He had not really been in a reasonable mood for

the last three days. Quebec's winter festival was different than anything Lorna had experienced. This morning, for example, they'd taken a calèche ride around the city, bundled in fur robes as their carriage toured the old Lower Town. Narrow cobbled streets were lined by century-old houses in the European tradition. Near the Château Frontenac where they were staying, the land plunged more than three hundred feet down to a rolling St. Lawrence River. Lorna, with her love of history and languages, could not have had a better time.

After that they'd watched the ice sculptors, finishing the last of their masterpieces before the contest and parade, working with hatchets and water pails. Ten-foot-deep chunks of snow became massive demons and fairies, animals and children. The sun shone down on a city turned into diamonds, the prisms of ice breathtaking, reflecting one off the other like a million precious stones. The crowds were delighted, sipping Caribou, as Lorna and Matthew were, to warm themselves. There was still time to see a canoe race through a river made dangerous by floating ice, and only when exhausted and freezing did they finally return to the château in the early evening.

And as far as freezing... Lorna really wasn't cold. Matthew had proved himself unreasonable about keeping her warm over the last few days. The white fur boots had cost him a fortune. Then there had been the outfit to match, then a dress in scarlet cashmere that she didn't need. The French dressmaker had wooed him from her window... So had a man who did charcoal portraits... So had a young woman who designed jewelry. If Lorna had had any idea before of what a spendthrift Matthew was turning out to be...

And the bath. He'd upended a half-bottle of L'Air du Temps in the water while she was undressing. Her entire perfume supply for the trip, barring the three vials he'd purchased that were too expensive to use. And until now, Lorna had thought that champagne was strictly for Christmas and weddings. She reached over to pour another glassful from the bottle opened solely for her, then leaned back, regarding Matthew through thick lashes, feeling deliciously decadent and thoroughly aroused.

His dark brown eyes had a sensual snap of fire in them tonight. Three drops of moisture glistened on his brow; a few more were still nestled in the furry mat on his chest from his recent shower. He'd just used a lime-scented shaving cream, and the faint smell lingered in the small, warm room; her fingers longed to test just how soft those cheeks were after shaving. They looked honey-soft. The towel draped around his middle would take less than a small tug to free.

His chest hair intrigued her; the matt was short and oddly bristly, and she couldn't understand why she found the feel of it so exciting. Perhaps because it was shaped like an arrow, a vertical line of it dividing his ribs, and around his stomach rather feathering out. Definitely an arrow, pointing down...

"Misha."

She glanced up innocently.

"We're here to ensure that you get warm. When you came in you were damn well blue." His stern voice lacked something in the way of authority; his eyes were dancing.

"I'm getting warm, Matthew." His unreasonable concern touched her, just as all his spoiling had touched her. She knew what he was trying to prove to her. It wasn't necessary. She lifted her toe to flick open the drain.

"Misha—"

She coiled her legs under her, and in one graceful movement stood up, water shimmering down over the natural hills and valleys of a very definitely feminine form. Lorna's instinct would have been to reach for a towel. Misha's was not. Her breasts were absolutely beautiful. Matthew's eyes told her that. He liked the way they tilted up; he liked their firmness; he liked their small, firm nipples. He liked the slight curve of her stomach, the rounded hips...

He wrapped a towel around her very quickly, not chancing her catching cold. In another way, he guaranteed her not catching cold, because the moment his fingertips touched warm satin flesh, all that formidable control seemed to leave him. She was snatched up to just that warmth she had been impatient for.

The chest hair rubbing against her bare breasts was as exciting as she remembered. Rough and soft, fierce and sweet. Lime and champagne and perfume; she was going to make her first fortune bottling that combination. More compelling yet was Matthew's own scent, surrounding her just as his arms surrounded her, just as his lips crushed hers, inviting her into their own private cocoon. Inviting? Insisting!

She was dry before he nestled her on top of the comforters and pillows. All her life she would associate the Château Frontenac with pale rose brocade and cream, with a mattress too soft and a comforter of down. So much softness, so much pale romance in the old hotel... while Matthew next to her contrasted to that. No part of him was soft. He was sure and male and vital, a primitive, lusty lover.

He didn't believe in inhibitions. All her life she believed a woman had a right to a few inhibitions. He was totally unreasonable...

"How I love the feel of you, Misha..."

She shivered violently. The contrast from languid, sensual warm bath to cool silken sheets was a minuscule excuse for that, nothing of any consequence. Matthew was working, very hard, to make sure she became warm again, beginning with the one small nub of a nipple he had between his teeth, dark and smooth, swollen and pouting for him.

He propped himself up long enough to study her breasts in lazy detail. "The other one has been neglected," he pointed out to her.

She flushed. There really was something disgraceful about the way her body responded to his touch. He worked on the other breast, while she practiced clenching and unclenching her hands on his shoulders. Then she spread her small fingers and stroked in slow circles down his sides to his hips, trying to pull him to her.

He was still angry with her over the scene at the airport. She could tell by the way he had made love to her over the last three days. Where she had the fierce need to be taken, he had languorously taken his time. He nibbled when she wanted him to bite. When she wanted to touch, he had selfishly given her all the pleasure. She wanted to drive him out of his mind with wanting. He had driven her out of her mind. Deliberately.

It *did* seem to even out at the end. She loved him far too much to let him always have his own way. She traced the muscles in his thigh with her fingers, applying pressure as she slowly worked the tense sinews. He groaned, most unhappy with her. His lips chased back up from her breast and captured her own lips again, scolding, paying her back with a tongue that flicked inside the warm softness of her mouth and drank from her sweetness.

Those hands of his! He never stopped. Palms cradled her bottom and pressed her to his hips. He was utterly possessive, and he knew exactly what she wanted. One would think he owned her hips. One would think it was his privilege to mold them exactly as he wanted, as if he actually believed he had some sort of sensual power over her...

No, he hadn't understood how she could have panicked at the airport. He was so sure that by spoiling her he could convince her of what they had. He was so wrong, her Matthew. He didn't have to spoil her into loving him. Perfection wasn't the key. He was a bear first thing in the morning; he had yet to discover how impossible she could be on the first day of her period. She didn't know exactly what had driven out the fear that love couldn't last, that her ability to love wouldn't last. Part of it was being with him, day and night, knowing what a complex man he was, knowing she could never uncover all the layers... Seeing the light in his eyes when he looked at her, never wanting that to be extinguished. Knowing he loved her. Really loved her. Not an image, but the woman with disheveled hair in the morning who loved sandals and Christmas and, yes, who occasionally needed privacy, whose temper flared up when she was tired, who absolutely resented not being mechanical... She loved him the same way. The champagne and the candles mattered, but they were the frosting. She knew Matthew. She knew the way he looked in the morning, and how he hated standing in lines, how he despised bullies, injustice, and cold roast beef.

It would last. They had love; they had trust; they had respect for each other. They knew each other as people. They knew each other's faults, as well as strengths.

And her heart lifted, defying gravity, when he touched her. She wasn't interested in gravity. Her blood sang when his hands stroked her hair, when his dark eyes bore into hers, cloudy with passion, glittering with need. *Dammit, you asked for this. I wanted it to last all night...*

From some distant world, she heard a ringing sound. His lips had captured hers, and their bodies were clinging, reluctant for the slightest separation. She arched toward him, an abandoned insistence that she simply wasn't going to take much more play. Since he was determined to marry her, she had certain rights... Her eyes were glazed and silvery gray.

Matthew was smiling, as she heard the ringing again.

"Misha. You're going to have to answer it," he whispered. "I won't be responsible for anything I might say right now..." He was positively gloating that she had to wait longer.

Her fingers fumbled for the phone beside the bed, her eyes never leaving his.

Desperately, she strove for some sanity as she spoke into the phone. "Mr. Whitaker?"

Her whole body stiffened, hands raking rapidly through her hair as she tried to listen. Matthew wasn't helping matters. And she knew he'd heard her speak his father's name.

"Chicken pox! But I thought Mr. Rudowsky..."

Mr. Rudowsky was a very capable, kindly, grandfatherly man whom Johnny had taken to instantly. He also wasn't really sure that Lorna needed to be called. He had decided that Mr. Whitaker should make the decision; the number for Richard Whitaker, Sr., had been one of the emergency phone numbers on the list Matthew had given Mr. Rudowsky. Mr. Whitaker had made the decision. Johnny was now at his house, with nurses around the clock. His temperature at the moment was ninety-nine. His doctor had been called and another physician had been consulted for a second opinion.

"Mr. Whitaker—"

Mr. Whitaker was disgusted with the entire medical profession. Johnny *itched*. There must be something they could do. In the meantime, he refused to stay in bed. In fact, he was right by the phone and wanted to talk to her now.

"Hey, Mom? Mr. Whitaker moved the electric train up to the hall here. Listen, I don't know what all this fuss is about. I don't feel bad. Did you know Mr. Whitaker could play chess? I already beat him once. He says I have a computer mind. Are you having a good time?"

"I . . ."

Matthew had the most devilish gleam in his eyes. Suddenly, his hands were seductively caressing her breasts. She tried to bat him away with one hand, while holding the phone with the other. She was fighting a losing battle.

"Listen, Lorna." Mr. Whitaker was on the line again.

Matthew's leg pinned hers. His chest just teased the hardened tips of her breasts as he grabbed the phone. "Dad? Give me Johnny." That was evidently accomplished. "Johnny, if you want or need us at home, we'll be on the next plane."

Lorna watched Matthew's face for a long time. But then, it was a long time before he hung up the phone. When he did, he settled over her, his eyes filled with laughter, her body filled with his, and her heart just as full of loving and concern as his was.

"Your son," he said softly, "has chicken pox. A very light case."

She knew that. She kissed the hollow in his shoulder.

"My father is beside himself."

She knew that, too. Her fingers chased themselves down his back, and played a blues rhythm on his hips.

"I'm sorry, Misha, but he doesn't want you home. He's got three adults waiting on him hand and foot. A TV in his room. The train. Chess players. He's got my father writing to someone he knows on the Supreme Court, something to do with whales. He's going to be perfectly unmanageable when we get back, Misha..."

"Your father," she suddenly said seriously.

"I told you he would come around. Didn't you trust me?"

She trusted him. Her heart soared with trusting him. They would have been home in hours if Johnny had needed either of them. She trusted that Matthew could decide that issue as well as if not better than she could. Johnny and his grandfather were perfectly capable of working out a few problems on their own.

She had her own to handle.

Her own had a shock of dark hair and snapping black eyes. Russian hands and Roman fingers. But then, the intricacies of language had always been her specialty.

Second Chance at Love®

All of the above titles are $1.95 per copy except where noted

SK-41a

All of the above titles are $1.95
Prices may be slightly higher in Canada.

HERE'S WHAT READERS ARE SAYING ABOUT

Second Chance at Love®

"I think your books are great. I love to read them as does my family."
— P. S., Milford, MA*

"Your books are some of the best romances I've read."
— M. B., Zeeland, MI*

"SECOND CHANCE AT LOVE is my favorite line of romance novels."
— L. B., Springfield, VA*

"I think SECOND CHANCE AT LOVE books are terrific. I married my 'Second Chance' over 15 years ago. I truly believe love is lovelier the second time around!"
— P. P., Houston, TX*

"I enjoy your books tremendously."
— I. S., Bayonne, NJ*

"I love your books and read them all the time. Keep them coming—they're just great."
— G. L., Brookfield, CT*

"SECOND CHANCE AT LOVE books are definitely the best!"
— D. P., Wabash, IN*

*Name and address available upon request